MAMAKO OOSUKI

Masato's doting mother.
Thrilled to be on a date with him!

MEDHI
No longer the classic heroine or anything, she's now just a dark-hearted bunny girl.

"It's our fault we're in so much debt!"

"Let's do our best to siphon all the money we can from these customers!"

PORTA
The youngest party member, valued for soothing the group's hearts even as a bunny girl.

"Mommy's a bunny, too! Hop!"

"We exchanged everything for chips and bet it all. And now look at us!"

WISE

With her magic sealed, she can no longer cast any spells. The world's most useless high school bunny girl.

"It tanks all your skills and luuuuck, so even Mamako is doomed to faaaail!"

SORELLA

One of the Four Heavenly Kings of the Libere Rebellion. A Necromancer prone to languid speech and sinister smiles.

CONTENTS

Dachima Inaka

Do You Love Your MOM and Her Two-Hit Multi-Target Attacks?

VOLUME 4

DACHIMA INAKA

Illustration by IIDA POCHI.

YEN ON

New York

Do You Love Your Mom and Her Two-Hit Multi-Target Attacks?, Vol. 4

▶ Dachima Inaka

▶ Translation by Andrew Cunningham

▶ Cover art by Iida Pochi.

This book is a work of fiction. Names, characters, places, and incidents are the product of the author's imagination or are used fictitiously. Any resemblance to actual events, locales, or persons, living or dead, is coincidental.

TSUJO KOGEKI GA ZENTAI KOGEKI DE 2KAI KOGEKI NO OKASAN WA SUKI DESUKA? Vol. 4
©Dachima Inaka, Iida Pochi. 2018
First published in Japan in 2018 by KADOKAWA CORPORATION, Tokyo.
English translation rights arranged with KADOKAWA CORPORATION, Tokyo,
through TUTTLE-MORI AGENCY, INC., Tokyo.

English translation © 2019 by Yen Press, LLC

First Yen On Edition: November 2019

Yen On is an imprint of Yen Press, LLC.
The Yen On name and logo are trademarks of Yen Press, LLC.

The publisher is not responsible for websites (or their content) that are not owned by the publisher.

▶ Yen On
150 West 30th Street, 19th Floor
New York, NY 10001

▶ Visit us at yenpress.com
facebook.com/yenpress
twitter.com/yenpress
yenpress.tumblr.com
instagram.com/yenpress

Library of Congress Cataloging-in-Publication Data
Names: Inaka, Dachima, author. | Pochi., Iida, illustrator. |
    Cunningham, Andrew, 1979– translator.
Title: Do you love your mom and her two-hit multi-target attacks? /
    Dachima Inaka ; illustration by Iida Pochi. ; translation by
    Andrew Cunningham.
Other titles: Tsujo kogeki ga zentai kogeki de 2kai kogeki no
    okasan wa suki desuka?. English
Description: First Yen On edition. | New York : Yen On, 2018–
Identifiers: LCCN 2018030739 | ISBN 9781975328009 (v. 1 : pbk.) |
    ISBN 9781975328375 (v. 2 : pbk.) | ISBN 9781975328399 (v. 3 : pbk.) |
    ISBN 9781975328412 (v. 4 : pbk.)
Subjects: LCSH: Virtual reality—Fiction.
Classification: LCC PL871.5.N35 T7813 2018 | DDC 895.63/6—dc23
LC record available at https://lccn.loc.gov/2018030739

ISBNs: 978-1-9753-2841-2 (paperback)
    978-1-9753-2842-9 (ebook)

10 9 8 7 6 5 4 3 2 1

LSC-C

Printed in the United States of America

Prologue   A Certain Boy's Progress Report...?

How are you?
   Fine.
   Are you sick or injured?
   Like I said, I'm fine.
   Are you enjoying yourself?
   More or less.
   I'm having a great time.
   Good for you. (Um, that's not a question.)
   Has anything happened recently that made you happy?
   The modest pleasures of regular level-ups.
   Aside from how happy you are to be adventuring with your mom, of course.
   Suuuure. (Also, not a question.)
   Is there anything you would like your mom to do?
   Tone it down... Actually, no, I'm gonna catch up with her soon, so she's fine.
   Would you like her to clean your ears?
   If the need arises, I may ask, sure, but...c'mon.
   Would you like her to cut your hair?
   Not the point.
   Is there anywhere you'd like to go with her?
   Look, is this...?
   What would you like for dinner?
   Meat's good... Wait a sec! This survey is clearly...!

The full-dive game Masato was playing, *MMMMMORPG* (working title), was the beta version of an online game the Japanese government was planning to release.

Being government run meant all kinds of red tape. Test players were required to answer regular surveys. In return, they were excused from school, so as annoying as it was, Masato always filled them out.

This time was different, though. They were being waaay too obvious about it. How could he not notice?

"I mean, look at it! This is… Oh, it's… I get it now."

He'd managed to put some sort of answer down on each line, and he couldn't exactly leave it hovering in front of him forever, so he reluctantly clicked the SUBMIT button and closed the window.

Then Masato turned and left his room at the inn. Time to investigate. Odds were high that survey came not from the government but from someone much closer to him…

…And that someone was waiting for him in the hall.

"Ma-kun, thanks for answering! I'm so happy! Hee-hee!"

It was Mamako. She had a pop-up window screen open in front of her and was happily reading the message on it. Believe it or not, she was Masato's actual mother.

By all appearances, you would never imagine she had a son in high school—she looked far too young.

"Well, at least you fessed up quick! You sent that survey, right? I knew it!"

"Yes, I did! I mean, you always answer those, right? So I thought maybe I should send you something in a survey format!"

"It's not the format I like! They're mandatory!"

"Oh, I know. Hold on!"

Ignoring his protests, Mamako ran a finger across her screen, "Okay, send!" she said.

There was a beep, and Masato received a message. "Mm? What now?" He opened the new message.

What kind of meat dish would you like?

A follow-up survey. What did he want? Steak? Burgers? Yakiniku and stew were both tempting, too…

Not the point!

"Mom! I'm standing right in front of you! You don't need to send an e-mail!"

"That's a good point. But…you took the trouble to teach me how to use it, so I want to make sure I actually do. Isn't it lovely when parents and children stay in touch?"

"I'm not objecting to you using the messaging system in principle! My point is—"

"Oh, I know! Hold on."

Mamako typed another message and sent it to him. Masato received another follow-up survey.

> I'll go out shopping for dinner soon.

Good…question?

"How am I supposed to answer that?! It's not even a question! Why are you so stuck on this format?! Do you have it set to a survey template?! Or are you just accepting any format suggestions the thing throws at you? E-either way—!"

"That's right! Let's send each other messages all the time! Every time I send one, I get so excited wondering how you'll answer! Hee-hee!"

"We can just use our words, though! I've already answered! I promise I'll reply!"

> Thank you!

"Noooooo!"

Mamako's e-mails came straight from the heart. The resulting chaos was how things always went for them.

What mother wouldn't want to relate to her beloved son using whatever new communication tool she'd learned of?

A new adventure awaited them both.

Chapter 1 My Mom Sees Through Everything (Except Her Son's Feelings)

It was the first night.

Quiet words were exchanged in a room at an inn.

"...It's just the two of us tonight."

"Uh, yeah. True..."

Masato had been keeping his eyes tightly closed, but now he opened them.

The lights were out and the room was dark. But the moon shone through the curtains, providing just enough light to see.

He could see, but he had no intention of looking at the bed next to him.

"...So, um..."

"What is it?"

"Uh... No, never mind."

Not only could he not look, he couldn't even manage a conversation.

Because he was sleepy? No. He wasn't the least bit sleepy. If anything, he was wide awake.

The two of them were spending the night in the same room—alone.

Just the two of them, along with that scent—body soap? Shampoo? Either way, it was the sort of scent men find appealing.

"...Ahhh..."

"...!"

The faint sound of her breath next to him. Very distracting. Her bed creaked slightly as she rolled over, and Masato almost jumped out of his skin. He couldn't handle this...

"Can I join you?"

"...Huh?"

Surprised by the question, Masato made the mistake of looking her way—and found her right in front of him.

Even in the darkness—no, especially in this darkness—the unnecessarily sexy, semitransparent negligee did little to hide her generous curves, which were right before his very eyes and getting closer.

She was clearly about to climb up onto Masato's bed.

Sharing a bed with someone this sexy meant... Well, you know.

Dad... Mom... This will be my first time. Soon, I'll be a man!

Was that right?!

"If you can't sleep, Mommy will sleep with you. Come on, Ma-kun, sleep with Mommy!"

"I'd rather dieeeeeeeeeeeeeeeeeeeeeee!"

This was no time for sick virginity jokes!

Masato leaped out of bed, pushing his mother away with as much force as he could muster without actually injuring her at all—so not that much force, really.

The lady in the skimpy negligee was Mamako.

And obviously, she was his mother.

"Mom, I beg of you! Please don't ever suggest anything so horrific!"

"Oh, goodness. You seem quite angry, yet you're being so polite about it!"

"This is a plea of desperation! A humble request from the heart! I just need you to understand somehow!"

"But you don't seem to be able to sleep, Ma-kun. Why not let Mommy spoil you?"

Mamako sat down next to Masato, hugging his arm.

Since the negligee fabric was as thin as it could possibly be, all her body heat, the soft folds of her— No, he wasn't enjoying it!

Masato was about to lose his temper and yell at her for real when...

"...Any second now."

He suddenly grew very calm and fixed his gaze on the door.

He'd figured it was about time someone burst in, but...no matter how long he waited, no one did.

"...Guess not."

Masato had been hoping a cliché would save him.

Just as he was lying on the bed, in the throes of awkward contact with negligee Mamako...

...Wise would suddenly burst in, get the wrong idea, and start yelling, "The hell's wrong with you?!" and then Medhi would show up and say something malicious while looking gorgeous.

Then Porta would come running, be super-confused by everything, and look adorable.

He was hoping that would happen.

"...They're not coming."

Why not...? Well...

The morning before...

The Normal Hero's adventure was progressing smoothly.

His party had everything under control. Their victory was assured.

As they crossed the field...

"Oh, monsters! Be careful!"

The party's adorable item crafter, the twelve-year-old Traveling Merchant Porta, spotted the enemy.

The monsters hadn't seen them yet. The advantage was theirs.

The first to attack was the hero, Masato... Or at least, he wished that was the case, but that was doomed to remain a wish.

The first to dash into the fray was, as always, the Normal Hero's Mother, Mamako.

"Leave this to me! I'll take care of them! ...*Hyah!*"

The sleeves of her dress fluttering, Mamako ran forward, a sword in each hand—Terra di Madre, a crimson blade with the power of the earth, and Altura, a navy-blue sword with the power of the sea. She swung them both.

And what happened?

The enemies were completely wiped out.

Rock spikes shot out of the ground, and a hail of water bullets followed behind, ripping apart the monsters before they even had a chance to scream. The entire battle lasted approximately five seconds.

"Hee-hee! I did it! ...Okay, Porta! Your turn!"

"Got it! Collecting gems is my job! Leave it to me!"

Defeated monsters dropped items that could be sold for money, and

Porta scurried around collecting these. The mountain of them was soon inside her shoulder bag.

Approximately ten seconds after combat began, all things related to combat were complete.

Such was the power of the hero's party!

Mamako's constant vigilance ensured the other combat members never got a chance to act.

Victory was assured!

Which left the rest of them...

""""*...Sigh... The weather sure is nice...*"""""

...all too aware of their place in the world. When the battle began, the other three combatants had settled down in the shade of a nearby tree, gazing off into the distance.

First, there was Masato. The Normal Hero.

"Oh... I feel like I just developed a new skill...and mastered it. A skill that gives me courage to claim I'm not just watching the fight but developing a new skill. Let's call it Brave Observation."

He wore a top-tier jacket that provided both resistance to status effects along with an auto-heal function (but didn't protect his state of mind). In his hand, he carried Firmamento, a translucent blade with the power of the heavens. He certainly looked the part of a hero.

To his right sat Wise, a high school Sage.

"That's nothin', Masato. As the ultimate Sage, I've learned Magic Observation, which is loads better."

"Oh? And what does that do?"

"Observe how I have nothing up my sleeve yet still manage to astonish the crowd."

"That kind of magic, huh? But there's no crowd watching you observe this battle."

As a Sage, Wise was great at magic. She wore a crimson sorcerer jacket, and was using her magic tome as a cushion—she was clearly not planning on actually casting a spell any time soon.

And on Masato's left was Medhi, a Cleric with a beautiful smile.

"You've both learned such wonderful skills. I myself have acquired Holy Observation and am polishing it as we speak."

"Ooh, even Medhi's joining in."

"So? What's it do?"

"It's an extremely sacred type of observation that purifies things in a sense. It can even straighten out the personality of someone as fundamentally twisted as Wise. Isn't that nice?"

"I think your spiteful side is what needs straightening out here..."

Clerics were healers, using Cura and support magic. She wore a pure white healer tunic that suited her job perfectly.

Clearly concerned about getting grass stains on her clothes, she had made sure she was sitting on what appeared to be one of Wise's camisoles. On the surface, she appeared perfectly pure and innocent.

Then:

"Oh, Mama! More monsters!"

"Got it! Leave it to me! ...*Hyah!*"

Another battle had begun. Porta spotted the enemies, Mamako's overwhelming firepower demolished them all, and Porta gathered the gems. "Over there!" "Got it!" "And there!" "Got it!" They seemed to be having a great time.

And the three of them just watched. That was all they ever did.

A thought struck Masato.

"...We can't just sit here chatting about random stuff. We've gotta do something."

"Uh-huh."

"Yes."

Wise and Medhi both agreed with him. They knew it was true. And yet...

"In which case, let's go with this."

Masato pulled out a flyer.

CASINO GRAND OPENING!

Below the flashy header were photos of slot machines, poker tables, and piles of chips. And a map.

Congratulaaaations! To the heroes who defeated Amante, one of the Four Heavenly Kings of the Libere Rebellion, we're offering a ten-million-mum giiiift!

*   *   *

There was a handwritten note that seemed to be weirdly attempting to replicate a habit of drawing out the vowels. Both the inexplicable acknowledgment and absurdly high reward were clearly suspicious, even by the standards of dubious flyers.

Masato showed them the flyer, to which Wise and Medhi said, "Yikes...," and "Again...?" respectively. Both of them glared at him balefully, but he held up a hand.

"Let me explain. This flyer was left specifically on the door of the room where I was staying."

"So it's bait? Another invitation from Shiraaase? Offering a high reward for defeating one of the Four Heavenly Kings so she can trick us into helping her with something else...?"

"Something that Mamako will end up resolving all by herself, while the three of us get nothing out of it. I've seen this pattern before."

"Honestly, that's totally my take on it, too. Fool me once..." replied Masato. "Well, we've learned our lesson. And yet...this might be our only chance."

Masato stared at the flyer again.

"See, I haven't told my mom about this flyer yet."

"You haven't told her... You mean, you think we've got a chance of claiming this prize behind her back?" asked Wise.

"Exactly."

"Mamako has total control over the party's money..." added Medhi. "And this is a lot of money, so there's a strong possibility she'd feel obligated to turn it down. But if we were to get the money directly, it would all go into our pockets..."

"Yep. We could split it evenly... I'm thinking of using that money to buy equipment and items to make myself stronger. I mean, you really can buy your way to power."

"That's, like...such a banal way to look at it..."

"Pay to win is the scourge of modern gaming, after all..."

"Yeah, but I say we turn that to our advantage. There's nothing wrong with that!" Masato insisted that this was the way of the world. He was very passionate about this.

"Third time's the charm. This is our last chance—everything's riding on this. If it doesn't work out, I swear I'll never pay attention to another flyer again. So..."

He bowed his head at both girls, pleading.

The two of them sighed, then nodded.

"Fine! If you put it that way, I'm in... Plus, if it works out, I'll be filthy rich."

"It's not that I'm displeased with the allowance Mamako gives us, but...it never hurts to have more money."

"True. Besides, there's a few cosmetics out there I wanna try."

"I've actually had my eye on this one outfit, and this kind of money would definitely help."

Despite their skepticism, both seemed pretty excited.

Or maybe just plain weird.

"Money... Mwa-ha-ha..."

"Money... Heh-heh-heh..."

"Um, uh... There's still the option of using it to make yourself stronger, but...uh, to each their own, I guess. Do what you want."

Once these girls were hooked on a dream (or desire), they weren't going to listen to a word he said. No mortal could resist the temptations of cold hard cash.

"Oh, and while we're at it, let's use that casino to take home even more," said Medhi, to which Wise replied, "Good idea! That's where we claim this reward, right?"

"Y-yeah. Superconvenient. Like, straight up telling us to flip that cash into the casino and walk away with even more money. Check it out."

Masato showed them the flyer again.

"Huh? ...Masato, gimme that." Wise took it from him and glared at it. "Hmm... Hmm? ...Um..."

"What's up, Wise? Something bugging you?"

"The handwritten part here... Is it just me, or does this seem like one of Shiraaase's invitations?"

"Probably. She did the same thing for the whole academy student recruitment event. Trying to bait us into it, that sorta thing."

"Right... But... The flyer this time... The wording sounds like her, but the handwriting seems totally different. Hmm… Eh, whatever. Maybe that's the point! Not worth thinking about."

"Totally."

Despite what she'd said, Wise was still staring intently at the flyer, but Masato ignored her. With both girls on board…

"Then let's go to this casino, claim that reward, and see how high we can build that stake!"

…it was time to act.

Leaving behind the inn town where they'd hit the nadir of grinding their time-killing abilities, they boarded a passenger carriage headed for their destination.

The party was bound for the merchant town of Yomamaburg.

The city was in the heart of an open prairie. It lay on the nexus of several roads leading from coastal towns to interior cities, and the amount of traffic passing through had made it every bit as big as the capital itself. It was one of the largest cities in Catharn.

One could hardly talk about Yomamaburg without also mentioning the casino…

…but that's precisely what Medhi did.

"Th-that's all there is to know about Yomamaburg. It's a place where business is always booming, so as long as you remember that…"

"Oh! …I bet they've got a ton of unusual ingredients, lots of options for clothes. We can get some quality shopping done!"

"Y-yes… Let's call that our main goal…"

"Hee-hee. That does sound exciting! You certainly know a lot, Medhi!" Mamako said, sounding impressed.

"Y-yeah… I happened to come here once with my mom, so…" Medhi was being very obviously evasive.

But Mamako's thoughts were firmly on the pleasures of shopping. She wriggled with excitement. "Mmph…" "Oops! I shouldn't move too much!" Porta was taking advantage of Mamako's lap pillow, so Mamako and Medhi were talking quietly.

Wise and Masato were sitting opposite, watching in silence.

"…Looks like she's on board for now."

"Yeah. No problem so far."

The three of them were enacting a secret scheme.

With Medhi in charge of distracting Mamako, Wise and Masato were whispering quietly among themselves.

"Phase one…get to our destination without letting Mom know why. Seems like we're gonna clear that mission, at least."

"But we can't let our guard down. I mean, this is Mamako we're dealing with."

"Yeah…and as her son, I'm pretty sure she'd be opposed to both the reward and the very concept of the casino. But honestly, even if we make it to Yomamaburg, it's gonna be real hard getting to the casino without her noticing."

"Don't worry. I've got a plan."

Wise puffed up her chest (or lack thereof). "What're you looking at?" "There's nothing *to* look at." "Okay, cool, now die." Her foot ground against Masato's, and his HP started slowly draining…

"Wise, Wise! Sorry! I take it back! So please, stop crushing my foot and tell me your plan! It hurts; it really hurts; I'm sorry!"

"Very well… So the key to conquering Mamako…is you, Masato."

"Me?"

"Of course! I mean, look, you just said, 'Let's go to Yomamaburg!' without a word of explanation, and she was instantly on board. You're our most effective weapon against her! She totally dotes on you."

"Oh… Well… I'm not really sure how to answer that."

"Oh? You're not gonna throw a fit, like, 'She totally doesn't'? Wow… Maybe you're actually maturing. Maybe your relationship has leveled up."

"L-look, I dunno. Does that stuff even have levels?"

It wasn't listed anywhere on their stat pages. Maybe it was a hidden value.

Anyway.

"Point is, Masato, whether or not our scheme succeeds is all on you. Be ready!"

"O-okay. I'll do something about Mom so we can pull off this casino quest… That does kinda sound like an adventure."

"Yes. A sneaky adventure your mom can't find out about."

"Now it just sounds pathetic…" He hung his head.

But it was an adventure nonetheless.

And one where he played a key role, one vital to the mission's success.

That felt pretty good.

"Right! Today I'll show you what I can do—not as a hero but as a son."

"We're counting on you. Now…time to get phase two started."

The prairie rolling by outside came to a standstill, and the driver announced their arrival.

Masato's battle was just beginning.

As befitted a merchant town, merchants ran the place; most work here involved buying, selling, and scrambling for profits. They'd expected entertainment facilities to be a modest side attraction.

How wrong they were.

""""…Wha…?!"""""

The moment they stepped out of the carriage, Masato, Wise, and Medhi's jaws all dropped in horror.

Everything around them screamed casino.

Instead of a sign with the name of the town, there was a giant billboard that literally read CASINO. The buildings lining the main street were all casinos. Even the blocks that paved the street each had the word *CASINO* carved into them.

Uh-oh. It was like the entire town was screaming that the reason they'd come here was the casino.

Masato's party was in trouble!

"Wait, wait, wait, wait!! This is bad, right?! The rug's totally been pulled out from under us!" he cried.

"Our adventure ended as soon as it began… What a feeble adventure it was…" Medhi lamented.

"H-hang on! We're still safe! If we can just keep Mamako in the carriage—!"

"Oh? Should I not have gotten out?"

As the three of them hissed urgently at one another, Mamako clambered down from the carriage and beamed at them.

Crap. If she saw all this casino stuff, she'd definitely be against it.

"M-M-Masato! Now's the time to put your power as a son to work! Hurry!"

"R-right… I'll do something…something…right nowww!"

Wise gave him a push, and Masato did the first thing that popped into his mind—reflexively, immediately!

He gently took Mamako's head in his hands, pulling her close. A tender hold.

Mamako's face was buried in Masato's chest, leaving her unable to see. Good, good. Now they were safe.

"Oh my! My, my! Ma-kun! …Hee-hee! This is embarrassing!" Mamako blushed.

"Huh? …Aughhhhh! What am I doooing?! Nooooo! My mom's turning red in my arms?! Eaughhhhh!!"

"Yo, Masato! Don't let go! Keep her right there! Keep it—!"

"So this is Yomamaburg! Wow! All these shops are casi— *Mmmphhh?!*"

"Porta, come with me. I've got something very important to tell you."

Wise took care of Porta, who'd started to say something the moment she stepped out of the carriage. With her lips pulled into a forced duck face, she was rendered mute.

Mamako's vision was sealed. Porta was being hastily briefed. They were safe…

Except.

"Welcome to Yomamaburg! If you've come here, you must all be after the casi—"

"Friendly NPC who stands at the entrance to town and explains things, may we have a word? This way?" *Smile.*

A man had unexpectedly showed up and started to say the last thing they wanted anyone to say, so Medhi quickly lured him into a quiet corner. She was definitely a beautiful girl. The man looked quite happy, wondering what he'd done to deserve such luck…

A minute passed.

He came back, abject horror on his face. He must have caught a glimpse of the deep, dark terror that lay beneath Medhi's bewitching smile.

"Kindly town-entrance NPC, will you explain Yomamaburg to us once more?"

"Y-yes! Th-th-the shops in this town are all owned by a company called Casino Holdings, which is why all the signboards have *casino* in the name, so though they may call themselves casinos, they are in no way actually casinos!"

He delivered this explanation through chattering teeth, then staggered away, presumably seeking some counseling room that could soothe the turmoil in his heart. Probably.

In any case:

"S-so, Mom, did you hear that? All the shops around here are made to look like casinos but aren't actually casinos! Apparently! See? Not casinos!"

"Yes, I certainly heard him. And gosh, Ma-kun, your heart is beating so fast!"

"Pretend you didn't hear that!"

Mamako was savoring the experience of being in her son's arms. It was like he'd hypnotized her—it had become quite easy to implant suggestions. Masato glanced at the others.

He didn't know what threat or dark power Medhi had unleashed, but she'd done good work. She gave him a nod.

And Wise... Well, Porta had a vague smile on her face and was shifting from one foot to the other, but this was so cute he wanted to give it the okay. Wise gave him a thumbs-up.

Whew... Crisis averted.

Masato relaxed, releasing Mamako from his embrace. "Hee-hee, Ma-kun!"

"Your daily quota has been reached," he said, pushing her back when she tried to come back in for more.

Well, here they were.

"Right, then..."

"Time for a lovely mother-son Yomamaburg sightseeing tour!" Mamako glowed.

Masato kept trying to move away from her, but Mamako just kept mercilessly pulling her arms around him. A Mother's Light made her shine extremely bright. "Hey, I can't see!" "Off we go! Hee-hee!" Excessive contact with her beloved son had clearly put Mamako in an unstoppably cheery mood.

As the glowing mother dragged her son ahead, behind them...

...Wise and Medhi were whispering to each other.

"Mamako's all over Masato. This is ideal."

"She doesn't seem to have eyes for anything else. I was worried for a minute there, but it looks like we might actually pull this caper off."

"Time to fire up the next phase. About that..."

"I got some good intel from the man at the gate, don't worry."

"Oh, nice, Medhi. Then we just have to find an excuse to split up..."

"Um, pardon me! Can I ask a question? It's about the plan Wise told me!"

While the older girls were whispering, Porta had mustered up the courage to speak. She clearly had something on her mind, but...

...Wise and Medhi each threw their arms around her shoulders, purring in her ears.

"We understand. Getting the reward and trying to double down on it in the casino without Mamako finding out isn't right," said Wise.

"Y-yes! So I thought I should say—"

"But you mustn't. You see, this is a surprise for Mamako," added Medhi.

"A surprise?"

"Yes, yes," Wise assured her. "We'll get the reward, and use the casino to make it way bigger, and then use that money to make ourselves stronger, and Mamako will be so surprised!"

"Normally, we leave all the fighting to her. We just want to relieve some of the burden on her, however slight... This whole plan is just us trying to make her life easier."

"O-oh, I get it! This is all for Mama!"

"That's right," said Wise. "That's what Masato said."

"Yes, he did."

"Masato said that? Wow! I knew he was nice!"

This was definitely Masato's idea, but he hadn't said a word about making life easier for Mamako. "He said, 'I'll take responsibility for everything!'" "He did indeed." "Is that so?" He hadn't said that, either.

"So you get it now, Porta?"

"Yes! If that's the case, I'm happy to help! If there's anything I can do, just say the word!"

"That's such a help... With your Appraise skill, perhaps we can figure out which slot machines or cards are ready to pay out..."

"Yeah, with Porta around, we're definitely gonna rake it in now. Mwa-ha-ha." *Grin.*

"It looks like our victory is assured. Heh-heh-heh." *Grin.*

Having thoroughly duped the innocent younger girl, sinister grins spread across both girls' faces. Their expressions alone ought to have led to their arrest.

While this was going on in back...

...up ahead, Masato had no idea that all responsibility for this caper had been thrust upon him and was just being dragged along, caught in Mamako's arm hold.

Then he stopped in his tracks.

"Wow, that's...a bit much."

At the end of the road, he'd found a casino that was so ridiculously gaudy it dwarfed all the other shops around.

Everything glittered. The signs, the building itself, the passages leading inside—everything was studded with magic stones that shone with brightly colored lights. On top of that, there was a visual display depicting a stream of coins falling from the sky. It was blinding. Gaudy without measure.

"This place looks way fancier than these other casinos... Oh, this is the one from the flyer... Huh?"

Masato checked his pockets, but the flyer was gone. Wise still had it.

He glanced over his shoulder and saw Wise and Medhi checking it over. They noticed him looking and nodded. This was definitely the place.

"...You guys ready?" he asked.

"Yeah, let's do this. The final phase!"

"Failure is not an option. We must pull this off."

They all nodded at one another.

Filled with resolve, Wise spoke up.

"Okaaay, then. I think this calls for some free time, wouldn't you say?"

"If you head west from here, you'll find an inn with three sevens on the sign. Let's meet up there this evening! How does that sound?" asked Medhi.

"Yes! I agree! I'll help!"

"Whoa, you even managed to talk Porta into it…! All right, let's do that!"

This was the moment that would decide everything. They had to get Mamako's approval here and the moment they got away from her dive into the casino.

If Mamako approved free time, then the casino was theirs to conquer!

"Mom, you agree, right? Just say the word and—"

"I don't mind splitting up, but I just think we ought to explore the place together first. I mean, it's our first time here, so that would be safer, right?" She smiled.

"Uh…"

That was a totally legitimate argument. Had they failed already…?

No, not yet! Masato dug in his heels. The boy who wanted to claim a huge reward and gamble with it would not be so easily swayed!

"B-but, Mom, hold up! Sure, this is our first time here! But we're not little kids anymore, so just give us a chance to stretch our wings…"

As Masato struggled, Wise and Medhi shot each other a quick glance.

"Um, Mamako," Wise suggested. "Let me be honest. The whole idea here is to let you and Masato have some time alone together."

"Masato just wants you to spoil him rotten, you see. Strengthen the bonds between you and him, making the two of you even more powerful," Medhi agreed.

"Huh?"

"Masato gets stronger when Mama dotes on him? That's amazing! How wonderful! I hope you spoil him so much!" Porta glowed.

"Wha—?"

"Gosh! Is that true? Ma-kun, you want Mommy to spoil you? This is like a dream! …I understand! Then let's all split up!"

"Whew, got Mom's approval. That's good— Crap, no it's nooooot!!"

Wise, Medhi, and Porta could go off and do whatever they wanted, but Masato was stuck glued to Mamako's side

That was a death sentence.

"Wait, back up! Where did this idea come from? Nobody told me!"

"Masato! Make sure Mama dotes on you a while! That will make her happy, too!" called Porta.

"Y-yeah, Porta, you're genuinely just doing this for Mom's sake, but—"

"'Kay, Masato, see ya! Go on and have Mamako spoil you to your heart's content!"

"We'll meet up at the inn with the three sevens sign this evening! Don't forget!"

"Wise! Medhi! How could you?! This is so wrong! What could be more ridiculous than my mom spoiling me…?!"

Masato's desperate protests fell on deaf ears.

Mamako had her arms tight around his arm.

"Hee-hee. Come on, Ma-kun, let's go. I'm gonna spoil you soooo much!"

"For the sake of my health try to keep it— Auuuuuuughhhhhhh-hhhhhhhhhhhh?!"

Mamako was over the moon; Masato was white as a sheet.

Their reactions couldn't be more different, but this spoiling was clearly inescapable.

They watched Mamako's glow retreat into the distance, Porta waving enthusiastically and Wise and Medhi in grim silence.

"Masato…we promise your sacrifice will not be in vain," swore Wise.

"We may have sacrificed you without your consent, but we believe it's for the best."

"Yes! Mama was sooooo happy! This is a good thing!"

"And we're free to hit this casino. All good things! Now it's time to—Oh, but first..."

Before they stepped into the casino, Wise slipped into a shadowy corner and quickly chanted a spell.

"Spara la magia per mirare... Transformare!"

Wise cast a transformation spell on herself. The crimson sorcerer jacket rippled, replaced by an all-new look.

Her flat chest was suddenly overflowing. Her waist tucked in while her backside developed an all-too-alluring curve. Her skin turned tan. She now wore a luxurious evening gown.

Disguised as an adult, Wise came back, showing off her new look to Medhi and Porta.

"Ta-daa! Well? Super grown-up, right?"

"Wooow! Wise, you've become the Queen of the Night!" squealed Porta.

"I have? ...Um, th-that wasn't what I was going for... I was just trying to look more like an adult, but...I guess she's the first person who pops into my mind when I think of a grown-up..."

"The Queen of the Night was your mother, right, Wise? I've heard the stories, but...this is downright brutal."

Medhi showed no mercy. She wasn't beating around the bush.

"B-brutal? ...Anyway, I might only kinda look like my mom, but I'm not her, I'm just a generic grown-up! This way we can act like we've got an adult chaperone with us!"

"This world is just a game, so I don't think they have any rule requiring one..."

"But just in case they do! ...And, like, if we go in as just a bunch of kids, we'll draw a lot of attention, and the Great Porta Plan will be way harder to pull off!"

"I suppose that is a concern."

"Huh? There's a plan named after me?" Porta said, looking baffled.

But the evil teenagers brushed right past it. "Oh, whatever, don't worry about it." "You needn't worry about a thing, Porta." "O-okay...?"

"Right," grown-up Wise said. "Let's do this!"

The three of them stepped into the casino.

Drawn inward by the lights of the magic stones, they found the entrance guarded by a well-built man in a black suit.

"Welcome to the casino."

"Thanks. It'll be just the three of us. These two are minors, but I'm their guardian, so they're allowed in, right?"

"Oh yes, no problem there. Our casino does not bar entry to minors or require they be accompanied by guardians in the first place."

"Ack... I was afraid of that..."

Wise's transformation proved utterly meaningless. There was a puff of smoke around her, and she was herself again.

"At least you're consistently useless, Wise."

"Oh, shut it! Let's just go in there and win, win, win!"

"Even when you lose, Wise, I will win for us. Not to worry."

"I can help! Let's all win lots for Mama!"

Not one of them doubting their inevitable victory, the three girls stepped inside.

It was definitely a casino.

The floors of the veritable pleasure palace were covered in red carpeting, the walls painted pitch-black, and the chandeliers above shone with all colors of the rainbow. It was as elegant as it was luxurious.

The casino boasted a broad selection of gambling attractions. Card and roulette tables stood in rows, and in the center of them was a massive flask-shaped machine for a bingo-like game called keno. Inside the flask were an assortment of numbered balls getting blown around and randomized by gusts of air.

There were also rows of slot machines—analog machines with actual moving parts and video slots with digital screens. Machines with three reels and machines with five—so many contraptions and so many varieties.

While there were no other children in sight, there was a large crowd of men and women of all ages.

Medhi, Porta, and Wise all stopped at the entrance, gaping.

"This is just...crazy extravagant..."

"Y-yes... It really is magnificent..."

"Everything is so sparkly and shinyyy..."

All three of them were left feeling a little overwhelmed.

Then an elderly gentleman in black came walking slowly toward them, a warm, grandfatherly smile across his face.

"Welcome to our casino. Is this your first time?"

"Huh? Oh yes! Our first time! We saw this!"

Wise held out the flyer.

The old man took a long look at it, his smile briefly wavering. But the warmth soon returned.

"I see. You must be the guests our manager invited."

"Oh? The manager here invited us?"

"We don't really know anything more than this...unless..."

"Is the manager's name Ms. Shiraaase, by any chance?" asked Porta.

"Mm? This casino's manager isn't named anything like that."

""""Huh?"""""

The old man looked puzzled—the three girls even more so.

"Oh, maybe she's using a different name?" wondered Wise.

"I suppose Ms. Shiraaase does change her name every time she assumes a new role."

"I see! Then surely she's using a totally different name this time!"

She could be annoying like that, so it was probably what was going on here.

When he saw they'd relaxed, the old man spoke again.

"I apologize for the late introduction. I am this casino's assistant manager. I've been given the task of serving as your guide, so I do hope you enjoy your visit."

"Yeah, thanks, dude!"

"Wise, that is not how you address someone of his status. Mind your manners."

"Sorryyyy. Thanks a bunch, *sir*."

"Mr. Assistant Manager! I don't know anything about casinos, so please tell us more!"

"I'd be glad to. First of all...as this document clearly states, we've prepared a reward we'd like to give you all. Would you prefer to receive the reward directly or convert it to chips to use in the casino?"

"So we can get the reward? Cool! Then convert the whole lot and let's take this casino on! Right?"

"Yes. I agree."

"We're here to play!"

"Very well. Then the reward will be paid in casino chips. May you all have a wonderful time. I'll be happy to answer any questions you may have."

The assistant manager produced a case full of chips from nowhere in particular. They were starting with ten million in chips.

Where to begin? The three of them looked around.

"Hmm… I say we start with the slots!"

"Ohhh, always an excellent choice. Using the slot machines to increase your initial stake is a classic approach to casinos. You certainly are well-informed."

"Huh…? Uh, I just picked something at random…"

"Wise, I think you just used up your beginner's luck," said Medhi.

"What?! Nooooo!!" Wise was horrified.

"That said, let's try out the slot machines."

"Okay! I want to try, too!"

The three girls ran toward the corner that was jam-packed with the slot machines.

Incidentally, there are two main types of slot machines: flat-top machines, which offer low but more frequent payouts, and progressive machines, which allow you to aim for a huge jackpot at very low odds.

The basic approach to playing slots is to start on a flat-top machine and slowly increase your cash on hand. This is merely common sense.

But our three girls were unaware of this, and lured by the high-value payout, they chose a progressive-type three-reel analog slot machine.

"How 'bout we make this a contest? Like, whoever hits the jackpot first wins. Of course, it'll be me, duh."

"I feel like this is a bad idea… That said, I'm definitely going to win. Heh-heh-heh."

"I'll try my best! I want to hit the jackpot!"

"To win the jackpot, you must wager the maximum amount of chips on all lines. The total chip number will show the amount of chips you've put in. You merely need to press the MAX BET button. Enjoy!"

Each put a single rainbow-colored chip into their slot machine. "Wait, we're starting at a million?!" "Each chip is a million…" "I feel so rich!" There were three scoring lines, and the max bet on each was a thousand...but the girls were too excited to realize how much that was.

Wise, Medhi, and Porta all pulled their levers simultaneously to start the process. A brief melody played, and the reels began to spin. Soon, they stopped! The results:

All three missed. Oh well.

"Eh, this was only the first turn. That's just how it goes."

"That's true. Let's go again."

"Let's keep going!"

So they did. Two times, three times...ten times...twenty times... Each time they drew again, but...

...the machines never once paid out.

"W-we're really not getting anywhere...which means..."

"Yes. I think it's about time."

Wise and Medhi shot each other a sinister glance, then checked to see if the assistant manager was watching. He was a good distance away, apparently observing the other customers.

This was their chance. They lowered their voices, launching their secret plan.

"Okay, Porta. You're up."

"For us to win the prize, for Mamako's sake—you can do this for us, right, Porta? Right?"

"Yes! If I use my Appraise skill, I might be able to find a machine that will pay out! I'll give it a try!"

All revved up, Porta started to activate her Appraise skill...!

But in that very moment: "Stop right there, patron."

A large number of men in black suits suddenly surrounded them.

"Wha—?!" "Huh?!" "Eek?!"

There was nowhere to run.

The wall of suits parted, and the assistant manager stepped forward, smiling just like before.

"I'm afraid our casino strictly forbids the use of Appraise skills or other means of determining odds. Should any visitors attempt to use such unscrupulous means, invited guests or not, there would be a significant penalty incurred. Porta, would you mind joining us in the office?"

"Yes, sir! I did use my Appraise skill, so I'll go right to the office!"
Porta saluted, readily confessing to her actions. Such a good girl.
Behind her...
"W-wait... Medhi... This means..."
"Y-yes... The worst possible outcome..."
Wise and Medhi had both gone pale as humanly possible, left staring into space.

But of course, Masato had no way of knowing what was happening back at the casino.

After leaving the girls, he and Mamako had wound up at a trendy café.

"Before we arrived in this game world, I would've never imagined the two of us out together at a place like this! This is like a dream come true, Ma-kun!"

"More like a nightmare if you ask me... *Sigh...*"

The idea had been to sit down a minute somewhere, collect themselves, and figure out what they were going to do next.

But moments after they'd been seated on the roadside terrace:

"Congratulations! You two are the seven hundred seventy-seventh couple to visit our café! To mark the occasion, we'd like to present you with this complimentary Love-Love Sip-Sip Drink sure to melt your hearts with sweetness!"

The waitress placed a massive glass on their table, with two straws that twisted through each other to form the shape of a heart. Clearly, it was designed for the two of them to sit face-to-face and drink it together.

A moment later:

"Hee-hee! We're so lucky! Come on, Ma-kun! How about you share this drink with Mommy?"

"There are things you shouldn't even aaaaaaaaaaask about!!"

Like sucking on a heart-shaped straw with your son, for one. How many deaths would that rack up?

Masato tried to protest, and yet—

Argh... I can't tell them we're mother and son, not a couple...

All the other people in the café clearly *were* couples. This was obviously a café *for* couples.

If word got out that he'd come here with his mother, that alone would be a disaster. Although Mamako had just called herself "Mommy," so maybe the secret was already out. He didn't think those giggles were just his paranoia.

They had to leave this shop as fast as humanly possible. His throat felt very dry, so first he'd drink some water. And get this conversation over with.

"Okay, so, Mom, as for what's next…"

"Oh, waitress! What's this Love-Love Say 'Ah' Pancake Set?"

"Pancakes served with sweet honey sauce. You take turns feeding bites to each other, and we offer a free service where we take photographs of you doing that and decorate the walls of the shop with them!"

"Oh, that sounds lovely! We'll take one."

"Don't order things that are even worse!"

The waitress bowed and left.

"Mom! Listen! We've got to figure out what we're doing next!"

"Oh my. Ma-kun, don't be in such a rush. But I understand. You just can't wait to have me spoil you."

"That's not it! That's not it at all!"

"Oh, it isn't? Am I confused again? Well, maybe we should go sightseeing with everyone, then."

"W-wait… Don't do that!"

Honestly, if they did that, Masato would be very relieved.

But he remembered what Wise had said.

"Masato, whether or not our scheme succeeds is all on you."

And how he'd answered.

"I'll do something about Mom so we can pull off this casino quest… That does kinda sound like an adventure."

Yeah. This was part of his adventure.

Masato had freely accepted the mission to keep Mamako at bay.

The girls may have picked the means of doing so without asking, and that wasn't fair—but then again, adventures were never fair.

I've got to sacrifice myself for the sake of my party... Man, that's really heroic.

He was duty bound to stick this out.

This was an adventure nobody but Masato could ever have.

For my party... Yes! It's all for their benefit!

It was a selfless rationale, one that wasn't in line with Masato Oosuki's true feelings, but he repeated it to himself until it sounded convincing.

His mind made up, he said, "M-Mom! I'm gonna make you spoil me rotten today! Are you ready?"

The moment his own words echoed in his ears, he could feel his heart sinking.

"How lovely... Hee-hee!"

Mamako's smile came from the bottom of her heart. A single tear escaped her eye, rolling down her cheek.

"Wh-why are you crying?! This isn't worth crying over!"

"Oh my goodness! I'm sorry! Mommy just got a little worked up. I was so happy to hear you felt that way... *Sniffle...*"

"O-okay, okay! I'm glad you're happy! So just, um, um...drink this!"

"Yes, let's. This is not the time for tears! Let's drink it together!"

"...Wow... I really stepped in that one..."

The Love-Love Sip-Sip Drink's heart-shaped straw was turned toward him.

His mother's eyes glistened with tears, and unable to refuse, he took a sip with her. It was...

"...Soooo sweeeeeet..."

Sickeningly sweet. So sweet it was actively painful.

And then Masato realized that all the couples nearby were staring at him. Every mouth hung wide open, like they simply could not comprehend a boy who enthusiastically demanded his mother spoil him.

It was intolerable. He couldn't go on like this.

"Uh, a-anyway, that's that! Let's walk a bit and figure things out! Let's get out of—"

"Oh! Ma-kun, look out! Behind you!"

Masato had bolted to his feet just as the waitress arrived with the

Love-Love Say "Ah" Pancakes. She shrieked, surprised by Masato's sudden movement. He blinked, and the tray went flying.

Honey-covered pancakes landed right on top of his head with a splat.

Fortunately, there was a staff shower room in the back of the café.

"I'm so sorry! I'm so sorry!"

"Oh no, it was my fault. I'm just glad you're letting me use your shower."

Mollifying the profusely apologetic waitress, Masato took off his clothes and stepped into the shower.

There was quite a collection of body soaps and shampoos for women inside—these must belong to the waitresses—but the sweet scent coming from Masato's head overpowered all of them.

"I'll just use whatever and get this out."

Then...

"Ma-kun, let Mommy help!"

"...Huh?"

The shower room door had opened, and Mamako had joined him. He was under the water and couldn't open his eyes, but he could definitely tell she was there. He was painfully aware.

"Wait, Mom?! Why are you in here?!"

"Why, so I can wash your hair, of course!"

"I didn't ask you to!"

"But today I'm supposed to spoil you, right?"

"Y-yeah, but—"

"Then why shouldn't I do just that? Just do what you did when you were little and say, 'Mommyyy, wash my haaair!' ...You used to hate washing it yourself and always made me do it for you. I really miss that, you know. Hee-hee."

"Argh... That was a long time ago... I can wash my own hair now...!"

There was no point in comparing Masato as a child to his current self.

But he'd put his life on the line and agreed to let Mamako spoil him. He'd made his choice.

"M-Mom! Can you wash my hair?"

"Yes! I'd love to! Leave it to Mommy!"

Shame, pride—they all went out the window. Masato let her take charge.

He just kept his eyes tightly shut. Not to keep the water and shampoo out but to avoid catching any glimpse of what was happening.

"Well, then, Ma-kun! Stand up straight! That'll make this easier."

"Okay… Uh… Whaaaa?!"

When he straightened up, something insanely soft pressed against his back.

Something belonging to his mother.

"U-um, Mom… You are…like, dressed, right?"

"Of course not! Can't have my clothes getting wet!"

"That's what I was afraid of."

His mother in her birthday suit.

Masato quietly tried to lean forward and extract himself, but she took a firm grip on his shoulder and said, "Don't move!" before pulling him back into the softness squeezing against him. Every time he moved, he could feel it shifting around his back, so he tried moving as little as humanly possible, but it was still there.

Soon the water stopped, and his mother's fingers were pressing against his head. *Scrub. Scrub. Scrub.*

"Argh… That does feel good… I mean, it feels good on my scalp, not my back! …And that's infuriating in its own right…"

"If it feels good, why get angry?"

"That's a fair argument, but… Argh…"

"Goodness, Ma-kun, what's wrong? Did shampoo get in your eyes?"

"No, that's not it. It's just… Argh, I'm ready to cry. What am I even doiiiing…?"

The tears were already flowing.

The brutal path of the spoiled had only just begun.

Once Masato's head was nice and clean:

"You got honey sauce on your shirt, too! We'll just have to go buy you a new one."

"Shopping? I guess that sounds relatively safe. Let's do that!"

And so they made their way to an equipment shop.

The interior was lined with armor and helmets. In addition to equipment designed for combat, they had normal clothes and underwear.

When Masato and Mamako stepped inside, the girl working there came over to them.

"Welcome!" she said. "Are you...boyfriend and girlfriend?"

"I *will* kill you." Masato glared.

"Eek?! You look like you mean that!!"

"Ma-kun! That's no way to talk to the poor girl!"

"I—I know, I know! ...Uh, she's my mom. We're just here shopping for clothes. If you say any other weird stuff, I'll abandon this whole hero thing and come for your head, so how about you just stick to providing information?"

"R-right, understood! Last thing I want to do is interfere with some mother-child shopping! If you need pant legs raised or have any questions, feel free to ask! I'll leave you to it!"

The girl darted away. This way they were safe from getting any awkward suggestions. A stroke of luck. Whew.

"Okay, Ma-kun, let's pick out a shirt for you! Yay!"

"Keep your voice down. This sort of thing is best done in whispers. We don't want to attract attention."

Everyone else in the store was a young adventurer. Masato quietly pushed Mamako toward the everyday wear, hoping nobody would notice them. Best to get this over with.

"Hey, Ma-kun, stand up straight. I want to see how this fits."

"Sure, go ahead."

Mamako picked several shirts off the rack and held them up to Masato's back, checking to see if they fit the width of his shoulders.

Masato maintained good posture, waiting for her to finish...

"This one's perfect. And it has antibacterial and deodorizing properties... Oh, I know. Maybe if I give it a good squeeze, that'll infuse it with love and affection? Hee-hee!"

"Uh, just what're you up to back there? ...Hmm?"

He had concerns about what was going on behind him, but something else caught his eye.

Over at the registers, the girl they'd been talking to was whispering with the other staff members. They kept glancing at Masato. Uh-oh... Was this...?

"Look, that boy's here shopping for clothes with his mom!"

"Begging her to buy him clothes? He's so spoiled! That's hilarious."

They were almost definitely saying stuff like that. Without a doubt.

This was bad news. When they went to ring up the purchases it would be absolutely mortifying. Retreat!

Masato turned to Mamako. "Uh, Mom, I can buy my own shirts. You don't need to pay for them."

"Don't worry, I'm happy to buy them for you. Today is my day to spoil you! If there's anything else you want, just make sure to tell me."

"That's not the point! That's not what I'm talking about!"

"Oh, isn't it? ...Was all that talk of getting me to spoil you just some sort of cover-up—?"

"No, no!! It definitely wasn't! It was, uh... I know! I feel bad making you buy everything for me, so let me buy something for you! How's that?"

"Oh my! You really don't need to. I mean, I'm delighted you feel that way, but...the money..."

"I'm getting an allowance, so I've got some saved up! Okay?"

Arguing like this was a waste of time. Masato quickly slipped around behind Mamako and pushed her forward.

They headed for the women's section.

"Right, let's hope they've got something decent..."

He had no clue what kind of design would look good on Mamako, so he just picked up something at random and looked it over. "Erk... Nine thousand seven hundred mum..." That was pretty pricey. Would be tough on his wallet.

"Ma-kun, it'd be a shame to spend that much money on clothing. Mommy thinks...*that* would be a better choice."

Mamako pointed at the bargain bin.

The contents of it were all priced at 777 mum—definitely pretty cheap. The bin was filled with cotton and lace, a mountain of cloth in all colors.

"And the price is a lucky number. Let's go with these."

"I mean, yeah, it's lucky, but…it's also pretty cheap…"

"It's not the price that matters, it's the feeling! Why don't you pick out something you think would look good on Mommy?"

"Uh, sure, if you say so… But what are these? Handkerchiefs?"

He picked up a balled-up bit of fabric, straightening it out.

And it was women's underwear.

"Whoooaaa?!"

"Okay, now go ahead and choose. Which one would look best on Mommy? Pick whatever strikes your fancy! Which one do you want to see Mommy wear?"

"I'm so sorry; please show some mercy. I don't care how much money I spend, just let me buy anything but this, please!"

He was ready to go down on his knees.

In the end, he had Mamako buy him the shirt, and Masato also bought her something. The same skimpy stuff she always wore.

"Hee-hee, a present from Ma-kun! I'll treasure these."

"…Yeah, great… Please do…" He hung his head.

He couldn't get the look the staff gave him out of his mind—a look that had clearly said, "Huh? You're buying panties for your mother? How screwed up are you?"

After leaving the equipment shop, the two of them began wandering at random.

"Hey, Ma-kun, it seems like all the shops in this area have different names."

"Oh, I guess these aren't part of Casino Holdings."

He'd been starting to wonder if this place was all casinos, but it was a merchant city after all. Now that they'd found the shopping district, there were stores of all kinds: equipment and item shops, stores that sold everyday goods and groceries, even hair salons and a hospital. They should have come here first.

Masato glanced up at the sky and saw the sun getting lower. It must be nearly three.

"Still plenty of time before we need to meet up… I guess we should find something else to do?"

"Yes. As long as we have time, I want to enjoy this mother-son date."

"Please stop calling it that…"

He'd said these words far too many times already.

"Oh, Ma-kun! I wonder what that is?"

Mamako was pointing at a shop ahead. There was a sign out front.

PARENT/CHILD… QU…T……… CLASSROOM

Part of the sign was obscured by the branches of a tree.

"Is that 'Q-U…T' part *quest*? You use that word a lot, right, Ma-kun?"

"Uh, yeah, I do…"

"Then I'm sure that place is for parent-child quests! Ma-kun, let's do that! The two of us together!"

"No, wait, that's definitely not what this is. The leaves are hiding the rest of the name and… Waahhhh!"

Unable to resist Mamako's most powerful tug, Masato was dragged inside.

The interior looked like a day care: cushions everywhere, a slide, a jungle gym, toys for little kids to play with, cute animals drawn on the walls.

There was a young woman in the corner sitting cross-legged, staring at nothing. Did she work here?

She noticed Masato and Mamako.

"O-oh? Um…are you a couple on a date?"

"I *will* kill you."

"Eek?! Is this a robbery?!"

"Ma-kun! You can't say things like that! …I'm sorry to just burst in like this. Is this the Parent-Child Quest Center? My son and I would like to take on this quest. Would that be at all possible?"

"Huh? He's your son? What do you mean, quest? …Ohhh, um… No, that's not… This is the Parent-Child Quality Life Classroom… Ah—!"

Just as the woman was about to correct Mamako, she suddenly broke off and looked the pair over carefully.

She immediately transitioned into customer service mode. A smile spread over her lips, and she greeted them happily.

"Yes! Welcome to the Parent-Child Quest Center!"

"Wait, you just said it was actually Quality Life."

"No, no, no, no, that was just your imagination! We've just rebranded as a quest center special for parents and their rather large children just like you! Yes, indeed!"

"Gosh, how lucky!"

"This ain't luck. Besides…"

Masato looked around.

There was a huge sign reading, TO SPOIL IS TO BOND! IMPROVE THEIR QUALITY OF LIFE AND YOUR CHILDREN WILL BE CLOSER TO YOU!

"Wow, that sounds incredibly dumb. So basically, this place is for little kids and their parents? We really don't belong here. Mom, let's go…"

Masato turned to go, but…

…the staff lady raced forward and took a firm grip on his arm. She seemed desperate.

"W-wait! Please stay a while! We've had no customers in days, and it's real bad! Ever since all the city's parents and children vanished, we've been at our wits' end!"

"Why should we care how your business is doing?"

"Please… It doesn't matter how old you get, being spoiled is important! Having someone who will spoil you unconditionally opens up the heart and enriches your life! And by doting on you, your mother experiences joy, as well! Both mother and son grow happy together! …Right, Mom?" she asked, turning to Mamako for help.

"That's right. Children getting their mothers to spoil them is proof of their mutual trust. Mommy wants to spoil you all the time, Ma-kun!"

"See? Come, come! Listen to your mother!"

"And this is the day when Mommy gets to spoil you the whole time. It might help if you learn how to get spoiled here!"

"What, seriously? You two have, like, a day for that set up? …Wow…"

The woman's smile never wavered as she took a step backward.

"Wait, don't get the wrong idea! There's a good reason for this!"

"A reason? Ma-kun, what could that be? Do you have some other goal in mind…?"

"No, no! I mean it! I'm, like, super into this! Let's study up on how to be spoiled! Yee-haw!"

He could not have Mamako suspecting anything. Abandoning all dignity, he wiped his tears and threw himself into it.

"Well then, young man. As a professional Doting Instructor, I can walk you through it. Let's begin!"

"Begin…what exactly? I'm honestly not sure what we're doing here."

"No need to think about it! Just remember how it felt when you loved to have her dote on you—when you used to throw your arms around her all the time, to get scooped up in her arms—and then just act accordingly. I'm a Doting Instructor, so you can take my word for it."

"S-so I should hug her? …O-okay, then…"

"Hee-hee. Come, Ma-kun. Let Mommy spoil you!"

Mamako spread her arms wide. Going in head-on was too much.

So Masato approached her back, summoned all his mettle, and gave her a hug from behind. Not a tight one—that would be too much—but a nice, gentle embrace.

"Oh my! Ma-kun, you really are such a spoiled little boy, clinging to Mommy like this! Hee-hee."

"Argh… Grin and bear it… You can do it… This is all educational…"

"And of course, rather than having the son take action, having him demand that his mother do something also counts as spoiling. Let's try that!"

"R-right… Um… Um… Um…!"

A flood of horrifying ideas rushed through his mind, all far too embarrassing. He could feel the blood vessels in his face ready to burst.

But he had no choice.

"M-Mom! Can I lay on your lap?"

"Of course! Right here!"

Mamako went down on her knees, patting her thighs.

Masato wiped the back of his head with his sleeve (he wasn't really sure why) and then put his head down on Mamako's lap, the shame of it driving him half-mad.

But honestly, his head felt pretty good. Soft. Warm. Relaxing.

"Ma-kun, how is Mommy's lap?"

"Uh, well… It's, uh…you know… It's your lap."

His mother beamed down at him, a blissfully contented smile on her face. It was the kind of smile that made you forget everything wrong with the situation.

But the instructor staring over her shoulder, looking extremely serious, totally ruined that.

"So, young man, how does it feel to demand to lay on your mom's lap at such an age?"

"Like I wanna die!"

"That's an unfortunate choice of words. It's like you don't really want to be spoiled!"

"Oh, Ma-kun? Is that true?"

"No! I'm super-happy! Being spoiled is the best!"

He just didn't care anymore. He forced a smile despite the tears.

"Argh! Instructor lady! What else should we do?"

"Let me see... Then how about adding story time to this? That's some very advanced spoiling."

"You're on! Let's do it!"

Masato hopped up and went over to the bookshelves. "Um... This one!" He grabbed a picture book and came back, putting his head back on Mamako's lap.

Then he held up the picture book *Momo-mom-taro*.

"Mom! Read this to me!"

"Gosh, Ma-kun, to hear you beg like that... Hee-hee. How can I say no?"

And now for story time on Mommy's lap! Here goes!

"'One day, a peach came bobbing down a river. A mother plucked it out and bit into it, and inside the peach was Momo-mom-taro.'"

"Now, son, ask your mom a question. Make sure to do so in a pleading tone."

"H-hey, Mommyyy... Wasn't Momo-mom-taro born from his mom like normal boys, not from a peach?"

"Yes, just like Ma-kun came out of Mommy. He's a normal boy."

"Hmm. That makes sense. A normal mom and son. But with a name like that, I'm worried about his future."

"Good job, young man. Now turn over for no reason and rub your cheek against Mommy's lap. That's really spoiled!"

"Y-yay, Mommy's lap feels so good!" *Rub, rub.*

"Oh my! Ma-kun! That tickles! Hee-hee-hee!"

Mamako looked unbearably happy. It was clear she was thoroughly enjoying this. The instructor gave a satisfied nod, as if the effectiveness of spoiling had been proven.

But Masato alone was forcing himself further into despair.

No, no, this is all wrong. It's all an act; I don't mean any of it…

Masato rubbed his cheeks against his mother's lap, his eyes glazing over, his mind screaming denials that reached nobody.

This was unbearable.

"Why does this always happen to me? …The girls are all off enjoying the casino, and I'm left here… *Sniff*…"

Lamenting the difference in their fortunes, Masato's tears stained his mother's lap.

As for Wise and Medhi:

"Crap, crap, crap! This is real bad! I'm outta chips! Hold up, hold up!"

"Wise, will you keep it down? I've almost got— Argh! I missed because of your yowling!"

They were teetering on the edge of a proverbial cliff, desperate to stay alive.

Clutching the analog slot machines with bulging, bloodshot eyes glued to the reels, they begged: "Aughhhhhh?! I missed?!" "Ugh! This one, too!" Yet it was one miss after another. The reels never lined up right.

But they couldn't quit without winning!

"We can't afford to rack up pocket change! We've gotta get that jackpot! That's the only way! All or nothing!"

"I know! If we don't hit the jackpot, we'll never get Porta back! So… Assistant Manager, sir!"

"If your initial stock of chips is running low, you're able to purchase more. How does that sound? Our casino does allow you to pay later…"

"And that means we can pay with the winnings, right?!" asked Wise.

"That's right! We just have to win enough that we never have to pay for it!" said Medhi.

"That is certainly a possibility, but perhaps you should calm yourselves and think this decision through—"

"Oh, don't fuss the detaaaaaails. You heard themmm. They just have to wiiiiin."

As the assistant manager attempted to talk sense into the two girls, a new woman sat down next to Medhi.

She looked to be a little older than Wise and Medhi. Curvier than your average teen, she wore a long black coat and was running her fingers through her long hair—which was of a dubious shade of purple.

This woman was gazing at the two younger girls through sleepy eyes.

"Um… Who are you?"

"Allow me to introduce you. This is—"

"'Kay, that's enooough. We'll have time for that laaaater… More impooortantly, you two seem like you're in quiiiite a pickle. What's wroooong?"

"The heck d'you mean, what's wrong? Our friend got charged this insane fine, and we've gotta earn enough to pay for it! …So, hey, if you know of any machine that seems like it'll pay out, please tell us! We're desperate here!"

Wise was clearly clutching at any straw.

The woman smiled, as if taking morbid pleasure in their plight.

"I seeeee. How aaaawful… Sooo what do you say to a little competiiition?"

"Huh?! What d'you mean? Like, against you? This ain't the time for—!"

"The rules are siiiimple. First, decide how much you'll waaager. Then we'll both play the slot machiiines. Doesn't matter what you line uuup, as long as you get a hit before meeee, I'll pay you ten times that vaaaalue. What do you saaay?"

"What? Ten times what we bet?!" cried Medhi. "Th-that would really help, but…but what's in it for you?"

"Does that maaatter? I just want to gamble with youuu… What do you saaay? We doin' thiiiis? Or nooot?"

Should they take her draaawn-out proposal?

"Ten times…" said Wise. "We could borrow a tenth of Porta's fine, and if we win…"

"We could get her back right away! I'm in!"

"Y-yeah, we've got no choice. Let's do this."

The two of them were still in a state of panic and quickly pounced on the bait dangling before them.

"Very wellll. I'll play you each onceee… Mwa-ha-haaa…"

For a brief, subtle moment, a faint glow appeared around her, like a skill activating. The woman smiled.

"…*Sigh*… Being doted on is exhausting…"

"Hee-hee! I got to spoil you so much today, Ma-kun! My body and soul feel so refreshed! It's like I've just learned a new skill!" *Glow.*

"Spoiling someone can't possibly give you a new skill, even in this game. Please don't even suggest it. And you're seriously blinding me. Could you not to glow so intensely?"

It had been a brutal trial for him, but they had finally left the Parent-Child Quality Life Classroom behind.

Out on the road, the sun was beginning to set. It was time.

"We should head to the meetup point."

"Yes, let's do that."

Mamako put her arms around him without asking, but he no longer had the energy to fight it. Masato just gave up and started walking like that. He had reached a level of burnout where even the sensation of his mother's chest pressed against him barely registered. Hooray for burnout. Apathy forever.

"Hey, Ma-kun."

"Mm? What is it?"

"Thank you for today. Mommy's bursting with joy now. I was so glad you wanted to spend time with me, and it made me so happy. Thank you again."

His mother's heartfelt, earnest gratitude caught him completely off guard.

"Y-yeah… I mean… If that's all it takes to make you happy, it's a small price. I guess."

Defenseless against this ambush, Masato felt his face get hot.

It didn't actually feel so bad…

Argh, she oughta be the only one happy right now. Why am I getting happy, too? Geez.

His internal conflict over wanting to retain his sense of self raged on.

...Perhaps it would take a lot more practice before he'd be able to just accept gratitude from his mother in earnest.

They walked on through the streets, chatting about this and that.

Eventually they found the inn with a sign that read 777—the place Medhi had chosen for them to meet.

"Looks like the other three aren't here yet... What should we do?"

"I suppose we should see if they have any rooms open. I'll go ask."

"Cool, thanks!"

Mamako went skipping off inside.

Masato leaned against the exterior wall, watching the crowds pass by.

"...Let's hope they all won."

He'd sacrificed a lot to let them hit that casino. There was no way that after all this trouble they'd come back like, "We lost the whole reward and went bankrupt! Ah-ha-ha!" That would be unacceptable.

So he was sure they'd show up all smiles, having pulled every trick in the book in order to win.

That moment was almost here.

"...Where are they?"

When he saw them, what should he say? He had to gripe a bit, at least.

Masato stared into the crowd, trying to think up the perfect phrase.

The sun had long since set. Evening had come and gone, and it was well and truly night.

Masato watched the road carefully, but there was still no sign of Wise, Medhi, or Porta.

"...This is far too late, isn't it?" Mamako said, worried. She'd been watching the crowds with him. Masato had long since run out of ways to placate her concerns.

What should he say? He mulled it over.

"Ma-kun, maybe we should head to the casino and get them."

"Huh? Oh, um... Yeah, maybe..." he started, and then it suddenly hit him. "Mom, how did you—?!"

"Ma-kun, be honest. They went to the casino, didn't they?"

"Uh, yeah… They did…"

"I knew it… The moment they suggested splitting up, all three of them started glancing at the casino, so I had a hunch."

"You did? …So you knew about it all along?"

"Of course! I'm a mother. We always know when children are hiding something from us. Hee-hee."

There was nothing accusatory in her tone; she just seemed amused by it all.

But then a look of concern crossed her face.

"Maybe I should have warned them… I figured it would be good to let them have their fun without me around, so I pretended I didn't know, but…"

"I'm definitely wondering why that consideration couldn't be extended to me."

"But since they're so late getting back, I'm sure something must have happened… Ma-kun, we'd better go get them!"

"Uh, yeah! Good point! Let's go!"

Fixing their eyes on the bright lights of the casinos, Masato and Mamako hurried ahead.

The casino lights were bright enough by day, but at night the glow was so overwhelming that it left no room for shadows anywhere.

All the casinos on the street appeared to be doing very well; the doors were wide open and customers were streaming in—some with evident delight, some with grim resolve, and some with abject defeat.

Masato and Mamako ran down the row of casinos, beneath lights so bright the stars above could scarcely be seen.

"Just so we're on the same page, Mom, how do you feel about casinos and gambling?"

"Well…I wouldn't say I'd forbid it outright, but I don't exactly approve, either. I mean, it sounds like gambling always leads to debt and ruined lives. You never hear anything good about it."

"Yeah, that's what I thought… And if I said I wanted to go?"

"I wouldn't stop you. I don't think it's good for parents to force their beliefs onto their children… But I might just hug you so tightly that you couldn't go anywhere."

"Physical restraint, huh? Love shows no mercy…"

She clearly cared very much about him, so this should make him happy, but instead he was just disappointed. Could you blame him?

"So, Ma-kun, do you know which casino they went to?"

"Uh, yeah. About that… Probably that one there."

Ahead of them lay the gaudiest, most luxurious-looking casino of all—the place the girls had been so clearly interested in when they'd split up. They were likely inside.

Masato and Mamako hurried toward it and found a large man in a black suit staring down at them at the door.

"Welcome to our casino."

"H-hi. Um…"

"This is my son, Ma-kun. He's still underage, but since this is a game world, is he allowed inside?"

"Oh! Nice job, Mom! You've actually learned something about games!"

"Hee-hee. Naturally! The guidebook has so many useful facts. Things that aren't allowed in the real world are allowed in here!"

"You are completely correct, ma'am. Mamako Oosuki, Masato Oosuki, our casino's manager has been waiting for your arrival. Please head on in."

"Um…?"

A surprise invitation by name. The man in black said nothing more but simply gestured firmly inward.

"What do you mean 'the manager's waiting'? Mom, we should be careful…"

"I'm so worried! Let's hurry!" She dashed off.

"Will you listen to me?!"

But she was already gone, and Masato was forced to run after her.

And so they rushed through the golden door reflecting all the lights of the street, and into the casino.

Slots, poker, roulette—all sorts of games decorated the lavish interior, each more enticing than the last.

And the staff working here were equally eye-catching.

The dealers handling the cards were cool and stylish, to be sure, but what really grabbed Masato's attention were the Bunny Girls.

Bunny ears, high-cut leotards constantly on the verge of overflowing, slim legs in fishnet stockings.

They were unbearably perfect.

Gulp-inducing Bunny Girls, right before his very eyes!

"Hey! I'm the ultimate Sage-turned-Bunny Girl, and here I went to the trouble of bringing you a drink, y'know?! And you only give me a one hundred mum chip? You've got some nerve! Don't be a cheapskate!"

"B-but I don't know what that ultimate Sage thing is…and I've been losing pretty badly, so I don't have that much—"

"Okay, start jumping. Jump up and down. If I hear any jingling, I'm chain casting an instant death spell on you."

"S-sorry! I do have money! Here! Take it!"

Crying, the man gave the flat-chested Bunny Girl a large pile of casino chips.

Masato was hallucinating. That was the only explanation. Bunny Girls were supposed to be all smiles and blown kisses, not menace and threats.

Look, over there by the slot machines! That was a *real* Bunny Girl!

"Ma'am? Have I seen you slapping the slot machine? Repeatedly?"

"Um, w-well… It refuses to pay out, so—"

"Count yourself lucky I'm the only one who witnessed it. If I were to report this to the boys upstairs, you'd be forced to pay a very stiff penalty."

"C-can we keep this between ourselves? Please?"

The woman at the slot machine handed over a large number of chips. The Bunny Girl gave her an incredibly captivating smile and poured the chips into her generous cleavage.

Masato pretended he hadn't seen that.

Okay, last time! Over by the poker tables, the *actual* Bunny Girl!

"Hey, cute li'l bunny with the shoulder bag! Gimme a good luck charm, will ya?"

"Okay! Leave it to me! …Will the card be good? It'll be a good card! A good card…here!"

"Let's see if it worked... Oh, that's a great hand! Thanks, cute li'l bunny! Take this for your trouble."

"Oh, okay! Thank you!"

He must be a high roller. The elderly man gave the little Bunny Girl a bag overflowing with wads of cash. Mm. Delightful!

Wait.

"Oh my! All these Bunny Girls look so familiar!"

"Yeah. Let's go hunting."

Since she was closest, Masato started with the self-proclaimed Sage Bunny Girl. He grabbed her by the bunny ears—perhaps not the best way to deal with Bunny Girls.

"Yo, Wise, what the heck are you doing?"

"Huh? Isn't it obvious? Serving these customers! ...Wait, Masato?! And Mamako?!"

"What? Masato and Mamako? ...Ah!"

"Oh! Masato! Mama! You're here!"

Bunny Wise's cry brought Bunny Medhi and Bunny Porta running over. Reunions! And that meant... "Ugh. Geez," Masato grumbled, secretly looking forward to a group hug.

"Mamakooo!" "Mamako!" "Mama!" They all hugged her.

"Oh, thank goodness, you're all safe!" She hugged them back.

"Yeah. I knew it. I knew it all along." Masato sniffled, lowering his outstretched arms quietly. This was how things always went. "Anyway, what's going on? Why are you guys dressed like Bunny Girls?"

"Yeah, about that! Listen to this! We—!"

"No, nooo! Stoppp! On-duty staff can't be slaaacking," a languid voice interrupted.

It belonged to a woman in a long black coat who looked a little older than Masato. She was flanked by several men in black.

The woman was twirling her long, purplish hair around her fingers, ambling forward as if she were strolling through a field of flowers, her gait every bit as languid as her voice.

Beautiful but with sleepy eyes, like apathy personified...yet she seemed to be carefully observing them all.

Masato felt vaguely anxious and was soon on his guard. He took a step forward.

"…Um, who are you?"

"Meeee? I'm the manager of this casinooo. Myyyy name is Sorella. Hiiiii."

"Uh, sure. Hiiii. So…what does the manager want with us? I heard you were waiting for me and my mom?"

"I waaaas. I thought I should explaaain directly why your party has all become Bunny Giiiiirls. Don't you want to knoooow?"

"Yeah, I think that bears explaining."

"Cooool. You see… But first, bunnies, do get back to woooork. Otherwise you'll never pay off that deeeebt."

Wise opened her mouth to argue with Sorella, but then she winced, shut up, and the three girls turned and left.

Masato considered stopping them, but it was probably better to get his bearings. He and Mamako turned to face Sorella.

"…Then please explain. And if you could talk a little faster…"

"Noooope. I won't hear any complaints about the way I taaaalk."

"Please, Ms. Sorella. We'd love an explanation. Why are they dressed like Bunny Girls? And what's all this about debt?" Mamako asked fretfully.

Sorella's eyes narrowed, focusing on Mamako. But a slow smile soon spread across her face.

"I'll keep it briiief… Fiiirst, Porta used her Appraise skill to find a slot machine that would pay ouuut. That was against the ruuuules, and the penalty was a trillion muuum."

"A trillion mum—?!"

"Geez, I bet Wise and Medhi put her up to that. Still, a trillion…!"

"Soooo then Wise and Medhi made a wager with me to get Porta baaaack. And they looost. So now they both owe a hundred million muuum."

"Both Wise and Medhi?!" exclaimed Mamako.

"Oh, that's riiight… Medhi was soooo angry that she kicked a slot machine and broke iiiit. Soooo including the destruction of property costs, I believe her debt is actually one hundred fifty million muuum."

"Aren't you the one demanding this debt be repaid…?"

"Yesss… Well, something like thaaat."

Sorella pointed across the casino to the prize exchange counter.

There was a list of prizes and prices, starting with ordinary items:

POTION: 10 CHIPS

MP RECOVERY POTION: 50 CHIPS

THOU DOST NOT WISH TO FIGHT WATER: 70 CHIPS

Next, there were other prizes and the number of chips needed to obtain them:

RUBBER GLOVES (ONE SIZE FITS ALL): 100 CHIPS

LAUNDRY DETERGENT (REFILL): 300 CHIPS

FOOD DELIVERY SERVICE (SINGLE USE): 1,000 CHIPS

And below those...

BUNNY WISE: 100,000,000 CHIPS

BUNNY MEDHI: 150,000,000 CHIPS

BUNNY PORTA: 1,000,000,000 CHIPS

...the three girls' debts were listed as well.

"H-hey... You don't mean—!" said Masato.

"Don't tell me you're offering the girls as prizes...!"

"I aaaam. If someone agrees to pay their debt, the girls are theirs for the taaaking. Until then, they have to work as staaaaff... Sooo what'll it be, Masatoooo? Mamakooo?"

Sorella allowed a spiteful smirk to flit across her face.

They had only one choice.

Masato and Mamako glanced at each other and nodded.

"Me and Mom will get the three of them back. That's the only option."

"Yes. We simply must!"

"Goooood. Well, have fun earniiiing! ...But oh, we're about to cloooose. So I guess you'll have to try tomorroooooow."

"Yo, wait, you're closing? This early?"

"You seeee, we've got special gueeeests tonight. We want to prepare them a little something speciaaal. So that's all for todaaaay! Off you goooo."

"Something special...?"

"Hold up. I'm not leaving them here. We'll pay off their debts, so at least allow them to leave with us—"

"I guarantee they'll all be safe heeere. They're valuable priiiizes. After all, Porta's with themmmm. We'll take extra, extra care of her-rrr. Soooo...see you tomorroooow!"

With that languid denial, Sorella and her goon squad left.

A moment later, an announcement came over the intercom that the casino was closing. It was still early, and the customers looked surprised, but they all began obediently filing out.

The staff quickly retreated as well. Their party members were mixed in with the other Bunny Girls. They all paid a cursory glance to Masato and Mamako and clasped their hands together apologetically...but all the two could do was watch them go.

Their fight would begin tomorrow.

"...I guess we have to retreat for now. Should we go back to the inn?"

"It's a shame, but I think so... We'll have to go back, book a room for the two of us, and get a good night's sleep to prepare for tomorrow."

"Uh... Then...you and I are gonna be sharing a room?"

"Yes. The first time we've slept together since entering this game world!"

Masato retracted his earlier thought.

His toughest battle was only just beginning.

"Hmm-hmm-hmmm, hmm-hmmm, hmmm-hmm-hmm-hmmm... Ohhhh?"

Humming brightly, Sorella returned to the manager's office, thoroughly pleased with herself.

But she found someone waiting for her inside the dimly lit room: A girl with a wild ponytail dressed in the same exact coat. She was sitting in Sorella's favorite executive chair without permission, her legs up on the desk, staring angrily at the casino flyer.

Sorella was a liiiiiittle bit put out but not mad. She didn't let herself get mad.

"Ooooh, ewwww, there's something gross in heeeere. How did that thing get iiiin? Where did my bug spray goooo?"

"Don't treat people like insects! ...There's no reason why I should have to explain, but I called ahead, arrived on time, and was led into your office by your own staff...!"

"Buuut, buuuut...all Mamako Oosuki had to do to defeat you was snap her fingers, riiight? You *aaare* an insect."

"W-well, I was careless, sure! I never imagined there were attacks I couldn't reflect! And she didn't just snap her fingers, she fired a laser cannon at me!"

"Ewwww, excuses are sooo pathetiiiic. I'm ashamed to be among the Four Heavenly Kings with yooou."

"Ack... Well, gee, sorry!" The ponytailed girl made a face and kicked the desk.

This girl—Amante—was fierce like a tiger. And she snarled at Sorella.

"The point is—! You sure lured Mamako Oosuki here pretty well! So hurry up and go fight her already! I'll help you—!"

"Whaaat? Are you a total iiiidiot? How could you possibly help, Amaaante? Get ooover yourseeelf. I've got this cooooovered."

"Don't just write her off! Mamako Oosuki's strength is off the charts!"

"I knooooow. But you seeee, if you fight strength with streeeength, you're just being stuuuupid."

Sorella paused to emphasize her sneer.

"Mamako Oosuki and her crew will be taken care of by meeee, Scorn-Mom Sorellaaaa, she who scorns all motherrrs. My special skill will take her dooown. I've already defeated Wise and Medhiiii. And all without even lifting a fiiinger."

She made her declaration apathetically, lackadaisically, but with unwavering conviction.

Amante clearly wanted to argue, but all she managed was an exasperated sigh.

"...Ugh, fine, be that way. I'll do whatever I want, too... I made a fair amount of money at Solo-Killer Tower to equip my lackeys, so I suppose I could top that up a bit in your casino...but I don't need to tell you that!"

"You really must stop overshaaaring. But we'd welcome you on the flooooor! Use up aaall your moneyyyyy."

"I'll be raking it in. Bye!"

Amante stormed out.

And the laugh Sorella had been stifling came bursting forth.

"Ohhhh, she's so duuuumb! With my skill, there's no way anyone could make any money heeeere! Not the customers, not Amante, not Mamako Oosukiiii! None of them will wiiiiin! Mwa-ha-haaa! ...Oh, I'd better make sure it's staaaacked."

One of the Four Heavenly Kings of the Libere Rebellion, Scorn-Mom Sorella, had already activated her unique skill. Now she was simply stacking the effect.

Imagining how Mamako would arrive tomorrow only to lose, Sorella hummed and waited for dawn.

CHUTES AND MOTHERS

1

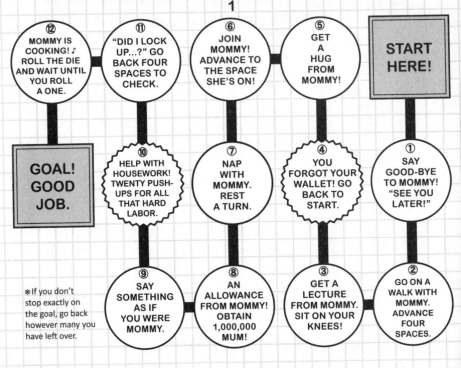

⑫ MOMMY IS COOKING! ♪ ROLL THE DIE AND WAIT UNTIL YOU ROLL A ONE.

⑪ "DID I LOCK UP...?" GO BACK FOUR SPACES TO CHECK.

⑥ JOIN MOMMY! ADVANCE TO THE SPACE SHE'S ON!

⑤ GET A HUG FROM MOMMY!

START HERE!

GOAL! GOOD JOB.

⑩ HELP WITH HOUSEWORK! TWENTY PUSH-UPS FOR ALL THAT HARD LABOR.

⑦ NAP WITH MOMMY. REST A TURN.

④ YOU FORGOT YOUR WALLET! GO BACK TO START.

① SAY GOOD-BYE TO MOMMY! "SEE YOU LATER!"

※ If you don't stop exactly on the goal, go back however many you have left over.

⑨ SAY SOMETHING AS IF YOU WERE MOMMY.

⑧ AN ALLOWANCE FROM MOMMY! OBTAIN 1,000,000 MUM!

③ GET A LECTURE FROM MOMMY. SIT ON YOUR KNEES!

② GO ON A WALK WITH MOMMY. ADVANCE FOUR SPACES.

 Let's all play Chutes and Mothers together!

 Based on these spaces... I'd rather not...

 Looks fun! I'll go first. So I roll the die, and... The heck? I got a four!

 Wise goes back to Start. I got... Erk... I also got a four...

 I got a one! Say good-bye to Mama! See you later!

 All right, all right, I'll do it... Anything but a five... Oh, a six! ...Wait, Mom's still at Start!

Chapter 2 There's a Sweetness in This World That's More Dangerous Than Any Sugar. Absorb Too Much, and…

Morning came.

When Masato realized he was awake, he covered his face with his hands before opening his eyes.

I just know Mom's face is gonna be right in front of me…

He might open his eyes to find her face inches from his, then panic and try to pull away only to somehow end up accidentally kissing her. And that would just be an unmitigated disaster. He had to take preemptive countermeasures.

He carefully opened his eyes…and saw the inn's ceiling through his fingers.

"…She's not here?"

Somewhat taken aback, Masato sat up. He looked around.

"Oh, Ma-kun! You're up! Good morning."

"Huh? O-oh, you're next to me. Mor— Nyaaahh!"

He turned toward the voice. Next to him was…well…

…a butt.

She appeared to be changing, and he'd caught an eyeful just as a suspiciously familiar pair of skimpy panties was pulled over her rear.

"Aughhhhh! Why are you doing that where I can see?!"

"Hm? …Oh, you mean these panties? Yes, they're the ones you bought for me yesterday! I wanted to save them for a special occasion… Besides, Porta's not here, right? And she's got all our spare clothes."

"Well, thanks for finding a good use for my present, I guess? Wait, no, I mean, why change when I'm in the room…?!"

"Goodness! We're family! What does it matter?"

"Are those the magic words that make anything okay?!"

"Oh yes, and for breakfast today, I thought we'd have *oyakodon*."

"Are you even listening?! Gaaah!!"

At times like this, it was useless to say anything to her. Masato was finally starting to learn this. Giving up was critical.

Now that Masato had gotten in his morning vocal exercises, it was time for breakfast.

Like Mamako had said, they were having *oyakodon*: chicken and green onions simmered, mixed with eggs, and served over freshly cooked rice.

Wasn't that an awfully hearty meal to start the day with? Hardly. Plenty of protein and nutrition to jump-start their sleepy bodies—one of the best breakfasts possible.

It was just the two of them today, so they took the *oyakodon* and soup back to their room to eat.

"I'm surprised this place had the right bowls for *donburi*."

"I was so pleased when I found these! Since I knew it would be just Ma-kun and Mommy this morning, I wanted the two of us to have a special meal together, and it just so happened that they had two bowls in the perfect size!"

"Hmm. I guess you're always lucky that way... Not the world's most spectacular form of luck, but still..."

As they talked, he dove into the *oyakodon*. "Mmm...definitely tastes like home." It just felt right on the tongue. Of course it tasted good, but there was something fundamentally satisfying about it.

But as satisfying as it was, it definitely felt like there was something missing.

Most likely because it was just the two of them. Eating alone like this, there wasn't much conversation, and the meal passed in awkward silence.

"...I'm always happy to be with you, Ma-kun. But this is a little lonely."

"...Yeah."

"I hope they all slept well...and woke up on time and are enjoying a nice breakfast."

"I'm sure they are. They're all together... Between the three of them, they're top-tier prizes worth 1,250,000,000 mum total. It sucks that they're being treated like prizes, but at least that means they'll be taken care of. I bet they're in a fancier room than us, eating a full-course breakfast or something like that."

"This prize thing is just not right... But yes, let's trust they're being looked after."

"Yeah. I'm sure they are."

He knew this argument was just to put their minds at ease, but he felt it was important nonetheless.

And Mamako seemed to get what he was trying to accomplish. She clenched a fist and pumped it in the air. Not a pose he ever wanted to see her do and one that was always mortifying, but...

But if she's perking up, that's for the best.

He relaxed a little.

Once he was sure she'd cheered up, Masato changed the subject.

"Right, so...time to strategize."

"Then let's head right for the bath! I'd better get it started!" She started undressing.

"I'm not talking about the whole naked strategy session thing! And don't strip here!"

He'd already seen far too much of the panties he'd given her, so he had her put them away again.

This was a serious moment.

"Um, first, let's be clear. We've gotta earn one billion two hundred fifty million mum to get Wise, Medhi, and Porta back."

"When you put it that way, it certainly is an awful lot of money."

"Yeah, we're not earning that much by grinding random monsters out in the field. And our weapons are both in Porta's bag."

"So if we can't fight for the money...then we'll have to hit the casino..."

Mamako's expression clouded over. She clearly wasn't a fan of gambling.

And yet...

"Mom, please. This is an emergency. The three of them are being treated like prizes! If someone else cashes them in, we're sunk. We need to make a lot of money very quickly. And the only place you can do that is a casino. So..."

"Yes, this most certainly is an emergency. And if there's no other way, then I suppose we have no choice... Very well."

Mamako nodded resolutely.

"Ma-kun, let's go to the casino together!"

"Yeah! That's what I've been waiting to hear! ...Oh, uh, not the part about going with you or anything, just to be clear."

But he'd finally secured her consent. Now he could gamble freely!

Cool.

With breakfast finished, Masato and Mamako hastily got themselves ready and left the inn. They were headed straight for the casino.

However, it was still very early. There was no one else on the road, and none of the casinos were open yet.

"Um, Ma-kun, I think we arrived a little too early."

"Actually, I wish we'd shown up even earlier... I have an idea, you see."

Masato hurried down the street, making a beeline for Sorella's casino.

Even outside of business hours, the magic stones had the place lit up. He looked the building over carefully, thinking.

We could go someplace else...but I feel like we should make our stand here.

Sorella's casino was the sort of place that would treat people like prizes. They were undoubtedly doing all sorts of other illegal, immoral things.

And that definitely meant they were cheating. Why wouldn't they be?

That was the point, after all.

"Right. Okay, Mom, let's sneak in."

"Okay, let's... Um, wait, Ma-kun? What did you say?"

"I said, let's sneak in... Racking up a trillion mum in debt in a single day is no easy feat. The casino was definitely pulling some tricks. So we're gonna investigate how and then use their own cheat against them. That way we'll easily rake it in. Good plan, right?"

"No, we can't! I am completely against it! We shouldn't do anything bad!"

"They're the ones doing something bad. Think about the predicament Wise and the others are in! This is straight-up human trafficking. There's no way we'll be able to win against people like that if we fight fair and square."

"That might be true, but for us to stoop to their level would... Oh?"

Mid-protest, Mamako suddenly directed her attention elsewhere.

It was a child—a little boy—dressed distinctively in some sort of old-fashioned ethnic garment.

He was running down the road, his eyes fixed on Sorella's casino as he followed the exterior wall before disappearing around back.

"Oh my! Ma-kun, did you see that child? He's too little to be all by himself... I wonder if his mommy and daddy are around."

"Uh, Mom, c'mon. This is important, so try to focus!"

"Oh dear. Oh my gosh! He went around back! I wonder if he's playing hide-and-seek? But I don't see his parents anywhere... I'm worried now. Let's go make sure he's okay."

"Geez. The second you spot a little kid... Moms, honestly! ...Fine, fine, let's go check on him."

They weren't getting anywhere as long as Mamako was fretting, so the two of them headed around the back of the casino to look for the kid.

But when they rounded the corner...

"Huh? He's gone?"

"I wonder where he went? ...Oh, maybe...!"

...a different building stood behind the casino. Along the walls were stacked a large number of wooden boxes, presumably containing casino prizes.

At the top of the stack was a small open window.

"What's this building for? ...The casino's warehouse? Rooms for the staff? Something like that? ...Either way, there's a good chance that kid went inside... Mom, what now?"

"We have to get him back! Let's go look for him right away!"

"Roger that."

This was working out. An actual stroke of luck. But he kept that opinion to himself, clambering quickly up the boxes and climbing in through the open window.

The window was set pretty low, clearly intended for ventilation purposes. Masato easily slipped inside.

Just what kind of room was this? There were wooden lockers all lined up in a row.

The child in question was nowhere to be seen, but the door leading into the hall was slightly ajar.

"A moment too late, huh? That kid doesn't waste any time. I feel like I used to be the same way."

"Aaand hup... O-oh?" Mamako seemed to be stuck.

"Sheesh, this is less hide-and-seek than tag..."

"Mm! Mmmmm!" Definitely stuck.

"Now where'd he go? ...And what's this room? It smells nice."

"Um, um, Ma-kun! Mommy's in trouble here. Could you please help?" She had tears in her eyes.

"Oh yeah, yeah, coming. I kinda figured..."

Her hips were stuck in the window frame, and she couldn't muster the effort to get the rest of the way in. "Here goes!" Masato said and pulled her inside. Rescue complete.

And then...

"We partied and had room service, and now we've overslept! We're so late!"

"You were partying, too... Ah, the changing room door's open! I wonder why...?"

...he heard voices from the hall. Female... On the younger side...

Wait.

"Uh...did she say changing room? ...No... You're kidding... That means...!"

"Ma-kun, look! There's Bunny Girl clothes in these lockers!" Mamako said, opening one.

"That's the last thing we neeeeeeed!"

Of all places to sneak in, they had to choose the women's changing room—and there were girls approaching that very moment.

If they ran headlong into them, that would be a disaster. Masato would be branded as a lecher and consequently arrested and executed.

What now?! What options did he have?!

He considered fleeing, but there was a strong chance Mamako would get stuck in the window again. In which case...

"O-okay, we've gotta hide!"

...the only possible hiding place was the lockers. Masato opened the nearest one and slipped inside!

A moment later, Mamako climbed in after him, like this made sense, and closed the door tight.

"*(Whisper, whisper)* Hey! What the heck?!"

"*(Whisper, whisper)* Um, I just thought I'd join you!"

"*(Whisper, whisper)* Whyyyyyy?!"

The locker was hardly that big, and the two of them were a very tight fit. Mamako's large, pillowy, um, assets were pressed right up against Masato's chest, and her hips and thighs were equally in full contact.

Enveloped in softness and warmth and scent, Masato's eyes glazed over.

...This is like...that torture device, the iron maiden...

The one that was like a coffin lined with spikes. This torture device wasn't actually stabbing him, but it felt pretty much the same. After all, he was waaay too up close and personal with his own mom.

As much as he wanted to scream and shove his way out, he was trapped. Someone had already stepped into the changing room.

"Helloooo...? Oh, nobody's here. Oh well! Let's just get changed."

The door closed, and he heard rustling sounds very close at hand.

It sounded like more than one.

"Ughhh, I'm no good at this Bunny Girl thing!"

"You're right. You don't really have the chest for it."

"Shut up."

"But we've got to make money! It's our fault we're in so much debt! We can't create trouble for Masato and Mama!"

"Yeah, I know. It'd be real pathetic if we just waited for them to bail us out. I mean, at least we've got our pride."

"Yes. Let's do our best to siphon all the money we can from these customers!"

"I still can't get over how you say crap like that with that pretty face."

This conversation could well get people in trouble, but more importantly...

...inside the locker, Masato and Mamako were whispering to each other.

"*(Whisper, whisper)* Ma-kun, is that...?"

"*(Whisper, whisper)* Uh, yeah, I'm pretty sure it is."

"*(Whisper, whisper)* Then it's safe for us to step out?"

"*(Whisper, whisper)* No, we'd better not."

If they stepped out now, it would lead to trouble. The girls were busy changing, and he was in a locker all pressed up against his mom. If either group saw the other, it would only lead to tragedy.

So of course someone else opened the locker.

"...Huh?"

It was Wise. Medhi and Porta were right behind her.

Apparently, Bunny Girl outfits were worn without underwear, because all three were stark naked.

Meanwhile, the heat inside the cramped locker had caused both mother and son to be drenched with sweat.

Both parties stared at each other in horror for a long moment.

Then Wise quietly closed the locker.

"We're gonna finish changing. You wait there."

"Damn, you took that well! Wait! At least allow us to make excuses! Or at least me!"

"The window's open, isn't it? ...And the two of you climbed in through there, heard someone coming, and quickly hid, yes?" asked Medhi.

"Yes, exactly! We're not up to anything weird!"

"Yeah, we know. It's 'cause Mamako's with you."

"Mamako would never do anything wrong."

"No such faith for me?! ...S-so, uh, anyway! Just now, I—!"

"You only caught a glimpse, right?" asked Wise.

"Some say if it's less than three seconds, you're safe," added Medhi.

"We're applying the three-second rule here?! Seriously, I feel like you're both rolling with this way too well!! Do you even recognize that I'm a guy?! Don't I warrant even a little bit of shrieking?!"

"I'm happy to see you and Mama again, Masato! Eeek!"

"Hee-hee. Thank you, Porta, dear. I'm glad you're all in high spirits."
Squeeze.

"Mom, this isn't an excuse to squeeze up against me even tighter!"

Masato had a lot on his mind all of a sudden. He definitely was not cool with his party just breezing right through this situation like there was nothing wrong with it. He thought everyone involved ought to be on their knees getting a very stern lecture, himself included.

But that would have to wait until the girls were done changing.

"...I see, so you were following a kid?"

"Yep. It was a great excuse to convince Mom to sneak in... Maybe I shouldn't admit that. Anyway, the kid left the changing room just before you all came in. You didn't see him?"

"I didn't... Medhi?"

"Nor did I. Maybe he ran down the hall in the other direction... We could ask the assistant manager to look for him later, perhaps?"

"You think that'd work?" asked Wise. "I mean, he's a stickler for the rules, but the guy seems nice enough. Seems good to me."

"I didn't know they had someone like that here," replied Masato. "Cool, let's do it."

"You got it. Let's just leave the thing with the kid aside, then... Masato, here."

"Would you like one as well?" offered Medhi.

The two Bunny Girls held out macarons with their best customer service smiles. "They're only one hundred million mum each!" "Mine are one hundred fifty million mum." "Put it on my tab." He shoved them both in his mouth, gazing around him.

They'd left the changing room and were in the three girls' private suite.

It was located within the staff quarters but felt more like the kind of thing you'd see at a fancy hotel. All the furnishings looked expensive, as did the paintings, plants, and decor. There were free snacks and drinks and even a pile of stuffed animals that at the very least probably delighted Porta.

"...Considering they forced you into debt, the treatment here ain't half-bad."

"We were pretty taken aback ourselves," Medhi said. "The assistant manager got this room for us, but...honestly, I can't help but think any time someone's being this nice, there's some ulterior motive at play."

"It's 'cause we're top-tier prizes, duh. At least, I think."

"And you're the cheapest of us, Wise... Such a cheap woman... You poor thing..."

"Oh, please. Yours includes compensation for the property you destroyed! The base amount's the same as mine!"

"Essentially, your prices aren't about quality, just your debts... You guys started with ten million split three ways, so...how did you end up like this? And I guess I don't need to ask what happened to that money, huh?"

"We exchanged everything for chips and bet it all. And now look at us!" *Ha!*

"It disappeared in a staggeringly tiny amount of time!" *Ha!*

"That's nothing to boast about! I was an idiot to place my hopes with you! ...Still, a hundred million? A billion? These numbers are nuts. It makes no sense."

"Yeah! Exactly! That's what we said!"

"The amount they demanded from us certainly was a lot, and I think the slot settings were off as well! It doesn't make sense for them to not pay out at all! I suspect they were cheating!"

Wise and Medhi roared like carnivorous beasts (not at all like bunnies.) Their bunny ears stood straight up from the force of their rage. It was a little funny.

"So they *are* cheating," Masato said. He'd suspected as much. "But honestly, I'm surprised to find you both working here. If they've swindled you, I'd have expected you guys to erase your debts with force and level the casino to the ground."

"Masato, I don't know where you got that idea, and I think we need to have a long talk about it."

"If I could've solved this with magic, I would have! But it's not that easy. C'mere, look at this."

Wise beckoned him over, and she kinda smelled good—like, did she actually have the nerve to have perfume on? Wow, who let her do that? But whatever.

She pulled up her stat screen and showed him…but instead of SAGE, her job was listed as BUNNY GIRL.

"See? Our jobs got changed."

"Changed… I thought that wasn't possible? That's what they said when we started this game anyway…"

"That's what I thought, but there you have it. They've been changed. I'm seriously pissed about it, but when they showed me the debt invoice, I had no choice but to sign it…and I'm not the only one. Same goes for Medhi and Porta."

"Even Porta? …Uh, wait… If your jobs have changed, then…?"

"Yeah. I can't use magic at all. Bunny Girl isn't a magic class. Any abilities we had before don't carry over, apparently."

"Wow… Wise, you're—"

"What's that, Masato? You're gonna comfort me? I guess even you can be nice some—"

"So instead of getting your magic sealed like always, you're now completely unable to use magic at all."

"When you put it that way, it's not actually any different. She's consistently useless."

"Shut up, Medhi! Nobody asked you!" *Raaage!*

Yikes, Wise was really pissed this time. It was pretty funny but also kinda dangerous, so Masato decided to back off.

"So, Medhi… You can't use magic, either, and Porta can't use any of her Traveling Merchant skills?"

"Yes. I can't use Appraise, Item Creation, or even the party storage! All our stuff is still in my shoulder bag, but I can't take any of it out!"

"Wow, seriously? Then I guess me and Mom are stuck without our weapons…"

"Supposedly, once we pay off the debt, we'll get our original jobs back… I'm not sure how much faith we can put in that, but with all this debt and the loss of our job-related abilities, the only option left was to do what we're told."

"Yeah… This is way worse than I'd expected…"

"And it's all our fault," Medhi continued. "I suppose it's not like me to say something like this, but…"

"Y-yeah…?"

"Wise." "You got it!"

Both of them stepped forward.

The bunny girls attacked!

"Please save us, O Hero!" *Wink.* ☆

"You're our only hope! Please!" *Smooch.* ☆

Wise activated Lucky Wink! Medhi activated Blown Kiss of Fortune!

Attacked by two Bunny Girls, Masato was captivated...

"Mm? Oh, sure, I was gonna do that anyway."

...Nah, he was the same as always.

"H-huh? It was ineffective?! Why?!" whined Wise.

"How come bunny girl specialty skills don't work?!" cried Medhi.

"Uh, don't ask me!" Masato said.

Maybe he just wasn't that into them? "You really oughta be more interested in girls your age, Masato." "She's right. You're being quite rude." "I could say the same to you two!" Neither of them ever treated him like a guy to begin with.

"Whatever... So...? How, specifically, are you planning on saving us?"

"Well, about that..."

That was the problem.

"I was thinking about finding out how the casino is cheating and using that to our advantage to rake 'em over the coals...but Mom is super against that."

"Yeah, go figure."

"It isn't exactly the most virtuous approach..."

"So I've got a choice between trying to talk her into it or coming up with some other plan... Wait, where did she go? I don't see Porta anywhere, either."

Masato turned around, searching.

Then the bathroom door opened. "Sorry to keep you waiting!" said an adorable Bunny Girl with a shoulder bag. She came running out, and Masato was all ready to catch her...

But this was not time to be playing around. A wave of horror washed over him.

"Sorry for the wait! It took so long to change!"

"...Yo..."

Behind Porta was another bunny...but not a "girl."

Slender legs encased in fishnet stockings spilled forth from the high-cut material.

The portion intended to cover the bust was entirely unable to withstand such generous proportions, and it was just barely clinging to the underside.

This was no girl. This was a bunny mom—Mamako.

"Hee-hee. See, Ma-kun? Look! Mommy goes hop, hop! Hippity hoppity! I hope... I mean, I *hop* it looks good!"

"...You gotta be kidding me..." Masato just groaned loudly.

"Ma-kun, you're so hoppity-harsh..." "Can't you just sulk like normal?!"

Mamako seemed to have her own interpretation of what it meant to be a bunny mom.

"Why does Mom have to be a bunnyyyyyy...?"

"Why not? Dressing like this here is a good way to avoid attention... I mean, however Mamako dresses, she's always gonna stand out. At least up top."

"Yes, I chose the biggest pair of ears I could find! Hop!" *Wiggle, wiggle.*

"I wasn't talking about the ears... Whatever. At least this way you should be able to move around freely."

"It makes sense for Mama to be with us!"

"R-right... Okay... I guess I can accept this as part of an undercover infiltration..."

Yes. Giving up was key.

Adventuring with one's mom was a constant test of a son's patience. How many times had he shed tears of blood? Once more, he wiped them away.

As he did, an announcement echoed through the room.

"All staff assemble for the morning meeting. All staff please stop what you're doing and swiftly gather in the casino hall. That is all."

Okay.

"We'd better make sure we're there, too," said Wise.

"They might take attendance," added Medhi. "So..."

"Wise, Medhi, and I all have to go to the casino hall!"

"Got it. The three of you go... Mom, what should we do?"

"Oh, I was going to join them! Hop! Mommy's a bunny, too! Hop!"

"Geez, you are *way* too into this whole shtick... I mean, you're making a conscious choice to say 'hop' after every sentence... You really shouldn't bother."

"Well, why don't you join us, Ma-kun? Hop?"

"If you're gonna keep up that hop-hop thing, then I'd really rather not... But either way, we've gotta go figure out how they're cheating, so...I guess I will."

With that decided, they started moving right along.

Only Masato was still in his usual gear, but that was fine. With the gauntlet and jacket off, he was just wearing a shirt and a vest, which kinda looked like what the dealers wore.

Three Bunny Girls, a bunny mom, and a fake dealer left the staff dorm for the main building and walked into the casino hall.

Since the facility had yet to open, half the lights in the hall were still turned off. The giant keno machine and the rows of slot machines were completely dead, giving off neither lights nor sounds.

A place where people game, eager to win...but where many tasted the agony of defeat. A sad sight, a symbol of a casino's dark side.

But enough wallowing in emotion. They mingled with the other staff; no one attempted to form lines. Everyone just gathered around willy-nilly, waiting for the meeting to start.

"Say, Ma-kun, I wonder if that boy is hiding in here somewhere, hop?"

"As long as you keep saying 'hop' I refuse to talk to you. Do not underestimate the power of an adolescent boy's rejection."

"O-oh... Mommy's all hoppity-sad now."

"You need to stop adding 'hoppity' to things. No one's gonna understand you!"

"Mamako, leave the boy to us," said Medhi. "We'll ask people to look for him. The staff here can handle that."

"Hmm... Well... I suppose we should leave shop business to the staff... All right. Please take *hare* of it."

Mamako seemed convinced. She let the matter drop. Whew.

But Masato himself was still pretty curious about that boy.

I wonder if his parents are working here…

Motivated by altruism, Masato quietly activated his skill.

It was a unique skill, possessed only by Masato in this world, or indeed, any world. A skill that allowed him to tell at a glance if someone was a mother or not.

…A Child's Sense…

A pale pink light filled Masato's vision, turning everything carnation colored. The light was coming from Mamako, next to him.

If a person was a mother, their body would give off this rosy glow, and Masato alone could see it. But Mamako gave off waaay too much light.

Right, anyone else…?

Using the skill, Masato looked around, wondering if anyone else might be the boy's mother.

Dealers, Bunny Girls, guards, chefs—the casino held nearly a hundred staff members…but nobody else had that carnation glow.

There are no mothers in this casino, huh?

Apparently so. Maybe there were some fathers, but he had no way of telling…

"Let's get things started. Good morning, staff."

An elderly man in a black suit had stepped up on the platform by the keno machine. "…Yo, Wise, who's that?" "The assistant manager." "Oh, so that's him…" Clearly important. Masato followed suit, bowing like the other staff.

"*Ahem.* Today, I'd like to start by introducing the newest addition to our lineup of prizes. This way."

Young men in black suits began carrying the prize forward.

It was a coffin.

"So this was discovered on the casino grounds. Inside is a mysterious nun. We assume she died due to a bug of some sort. There was a proposal to take her to the church to be revived, but that would cost money, so instead we've decided to dispose of her by offering her as a prize. She's available for a single mum chip. As this is a prize we wish to rid ourselves of posthaste, we have no issues with any staff member trading for her. Please do!"

Well, there you had it.

Masato hung his head.

"Less a prize for selective tastes than one specifically for us... Any time we find a coffin, you-know-who's inside..."

"Yeah...no point even wondering... She wasn't the manager here; she was the prize..." said Wise.

"I feel like she's staring at us from inside that thing, even though that isn't possible..." said Medhi.

"I'll trade for her later! Leave it to me!"

"Thank you, Porta. We'd better secure her quick, hop."

She'd already been carried away somewhere, but for now, it was best to forget about her.

The assistant manager went over the rest of the business for the day, and then...

"And now, a word from our manager."

He bowed and left the stage.

Replacing him was the casino's manager, Sorella.

"Morniiiing. I'm Sorellaaaa. How's everyone doooing?"

Even at a business meeting, she maintained that same languid speaking style. She looked around the room.

Masato quickly shrank out of sight. He and Mamako definitely didn't belong here. They couldn't let themselves be seen.

"Oh my! Ma-kun, what's wrong? Does your tummy hurt?"

"No! Mom, hide! Quick!"

Masato quickly grabbed Mamako's shoulders, pulling her down. Safely out of sight, he glanced around to see if they'd been spotted.

And Sorella...

"Ummm... Today we have some special guests comiiiing... So do your best, everyooone. Make it seem like we're a kind, friendly, totally not suspicious casino, okaaay? Goood, then it's time to ooopen."

...simply addressed her staff and languidly walked away.

It seemed that Masato and Mamako had gone unnoticed.

"Whew, that was close..."

"Hee-hee. Ma-kun's letting Mommy spoil him again today! I'm so glad the Quality Life Classroom taught us how."

"That's not what's going on!"

He quickly pulled his hands off her shoulders.

It was time for the casino to open.

The staff moved quickly, bouncers and dealers hurrying off to their positions.

The Bunny Girls—Wise, Medhi, and Porta included—lined up by the doors, ready to greet the customers.

All the lights came on, and the slots began to hum. Sound and light transformed the place into a den of pleasure, hope, greed, joy, and sorrow.

As he watched the customers pour in, Masato sighed.

"Sheesh. We never got a chance to figure out how they were cheating… Oh well. At least Sorella and the other staff didn't notice us. I guess I'll poke around a bit and pretend to work."

"Ma-kun, don't do anything naughty. Promise Mommy you won't."

"Yeah, yeah, I know."

"Yeees, Masatoooo. Don't be naaaughty."

"Yeah, yeah, I already promised… Wait. Augh!!"

Sorella was standing right next to him.

"H-how…?!"

"Mwa-haaa. You thought I didn't notiiice? It was sooo obvioous. Too baaad."

"Seriously…? Gah…"

"I don't mind you sneaking iiin; don't woooorry. The casino's open anywaaay. Go ahead and plaaay. Sooo…"

Sorella snapped her fingers.

A Bunny Girl came over and handed Masato a case of chips. He opened the lid to see chips of several colors all lined up in rows of ten.

"Fair enough. Can't exactly gamble without chips… Lessee what we got here…"

The colors and values were as follows:

Red: 50 mum

Green: 250 mum
Black: 1,000 mum
Purple: 5,000 mum
Yellow: 10,000 mum
Brown: 50,000 mum
Orange: 250,000 mum
Gold: 500,000 mum
Rainbow: 1,000,000 mum

Masato picked up a rainbow chip, his fingers shaking.

"U-um... This ridiculous value is..."

"So, for instaaance, the red chips are worth fifty mum, seee? Which meeeeans... Well, you knoooow."

"One mum is, like, one yen, so..."

There were ten of each chip, making this case worth a total of 18,163,000 yen.

The blood drained from Masato's face. Meanwhile, Sorella seemed highly amused.

"We let you pay laaaater. Go ahead and use thooose."

"No way! You can't just give people eighteen million and tell them to go have fun! T-take these back! I'm not accepting them!"

"Whyyy? I meeeean, if you don't have chiiips, you can't plaaay. You need funds to get your party baaack. Isn't that the poiiiiint?"

"I-it is, but...but this is..."

Masato stared down at the case of chips, flustered.

Then:

"Ma-kun! Over here! Mommy's in a bit of a pinch!"

Mamako was calling his name. He looked around.

She was surrounded by customers.

"What a beautiful Bunny Girl! Please show us your Lucky Wink! I could use a little fortune!"

"I-I'm so sorry. I don't work here...and I'm not a girl, I'm a mother. So..."

"Whaaat?! You're far too young and beautiful to be a mother! Hang on, so you're a bunny mom?! That's a super-rare kind of bunny! Well, all the more reason, then! I'll pay you! Please! Gimme a wink!"

"If you insist, I suppose it would be rude not to... Well... *Hyah!*"

Mamako winked! Lucky Mom Wink ☆

And with that: "Oh! I can feel my luck skyrocketing!" "Really? Then let me!" "Me too!" "And me!" Whatever the actual effect, regular customers and high rollers alike were swarming around Mamako, demanding winks, and she dutifully doled them out.

A minute later:

The crowd passed, and Mamako was left holding a pile of chips as payment—about twice the number in the case Masato held.

Sorella's jaw dropped.

"Wh-whaaat?! You collected chips without borrowiiiing?!"

"Geez, she's something, huh? My own mother terrifies even me... So!"

Masato put the case of chips back in Sorella's hands and headed toward Mamako.

"Uh, Mom, mind if we split those chips?"

"Oh my! You want some? Okay! Half for Ma-kun, and half for Mommy!"

"L-look, just so we're clear, I'm not asking to be spoiled! If we have chips, that means we don't need to take out a loan. Understand?"

"Ma-kun, you protest too much! Hee-hee."

No, no! That wasn't what this was! He was just being rational!

But with chips in hand, it was time for the battle to begin.

Masato considered getting the Bunny Girls he knew to help him sort the chips Mamako had collected, but there was no sign of them. Wise, Medhi, and Porta had all gone off somewhere. They were on the clock, after all.

Another Bunny Girl came over and consolidated the chips for them in two cases, one for Masato, one for Mamako. Minus a few for her tip.

Now then, what to try first?

"There's a whole lot here... So let's start with Texas Hold'em."

There was a round poker table right next to him.

It was a high-limit table, with a big blind of 100,000.

"That seems a bit crazy...but you can't win if you don't play. All right."

There were seats for ten people. Masato sat down, folded his legs elegantly, and tried to look like a gambler.

Mamako tried to sit down next to him.

"Hang on. If you're gonna play, too, Mom, you should play at a different table."

"Oh, why? I want to play with you, Ma-kun!"

"I'm not saying this to be mean, okay? Texas Hold'em is a game where each player is competing against the others. What's the use of us fighting each other?"

"Gosh, is that right? ...You sure know a lot, Ma-kun."

"It's 'cause I've played it online before. I know the basics, at least."

"Well, okay. Then Mommy will just watch you play—"

"Parental participation is strictly forbidden... You said you were just gonna watch me in class at that school, too, but you couldn't help yourself, remember? Mom, you know you're gonna end up joining in somehow, and that'll really hurt us here. So please go find something else to do."

"I don't want to get in your way, Ma-kun... Well, all right. I can't be here bothering you, so I'll just take a walk around the casino."

Mamako looked a little sad but went off in the other direction, her bunny ears drooping.

Masato felt a little guilty, but he had to do it. There was no point in having Mamako steal all Masato's chips. He put it out of his mind.

Right.

"Now I've just gotta get a few more players... Hopefully some gather soon."

"Ohhhh? Then I don't mind if I doooo."

And here was Sorella again, taking a seat opposite Masato.

"Seems a waste not tooooo. What about a one-on-one maaatch? Or are you too scaaaared?"

"Course I'm not."

"Reaaaally? ...You knoooow... I'm aaactually...one of the Four Heavenly Kings of the Libere Rebellion, Scorn-Mom Sorella, she who scorns the very concept of mooooothers. Are you scared nooooow?"

"...Huh?"

The woman running her hands through her oddly colored hair, gazing at him with sleepy eyes, was none other than...

...the second major foe from the group they'd been fighting.

"Scorn-Mom Sorella...? You're...one of the Four Heavenly Kings?"

"Yes, I aaam. Surpriiiised? I bet you aaaaare. Thanks for falling for that flyer I seeeeent. Mwa-ha-haaaa."

"You mean...that casino flyer was...? ...Oh."

"That's riiiiiight. An invitation from your enemyyyyy... So what noooow? Wanna take me ooooon? You see, I don't believe in fighting with magic or swooooords. I only fight by gaaaambling. What d'you saaaay?"

"Wow, facing off against one of the Four Heavenly Kings already... W-well, I dunno if you're telling the truth, but I won't back down from a challenge! I'm not so easily frightened. No point in trying to rattle me!"

"Ohhh? Well, aren't you a heroooo. Let's do thiiis! Mwa-ha-haaaa."

And as Sorella laughed to herself...

"Mm? ...Just now, was that...?"

...Masato felt like her body had briefly glowed, albeit in a different color from Mamako's A Mother's Light.

But everywhere he looked, the casino hall was full of lights. Perhaps it was due to a glint from the magic stones. Masato decided that was more likely.

"Then let's begiiiin. Are you readyyyy?"

"Yep! Let's do this! I'm ready to win!"

Sorella slid a tile with a *D* on it toward Masato.

Whichever seat held this stone—the Dealer Button—would serve as the dealer. That was the rule.

Masato took a deck of cards from a Bunny Girl and shuffled as elegantly as he could. Fifty-two cards, no joker.

"Two-person Texas Hold'em... Here goes!"

The game consisted of four rounds of betting.

The first round was called the pre-flop.

"No cheating, okaaay?"

"Of course not."

As the dealer, Masato dealt two cards facedown before each of them.

The rest of the cards went in a deck in the center of the table. Each checked their hand, raising just the edges of the cards so their opponent couldn't see.

Masato's hand was a seven of spades and a king of diamonds.

"Hmm, I see… Then first, the forced bets."

"Since it's just the two of us, and you're the deaaaaler…you pay the small bliiiind. I'll pay the big bliiiind."

The small blind was half the table's minimum bet and the big blind the full value. Those were the rules.

Masato tossed in a brown 50,000-mum chip. Sorella offered two of the same.

Now it was time to think. Masato consulted his hand.

A seven of spades and a king of diamonds… Should I fight with those or fold?

This game proceeded to the next round of play once each participant's bets were the same value.

Masato made up his mind.

"…Call."

Calling a bet meant paying the same value as the current bet—essentially, electing to continue the game. Masato added another brown chip. If he'd decided not to continue playing the hand, he would have said, "Fold." Chips already paid were gone for good; only the game's winner would collect.

But since Masato had called, the game continued.

The total value of chips on the table was now 200,000 mum.

Now for the second round of betting, the "flop."

"Hurry uuuup, deeeealer!"

"I know! Don't rush me!"

Masato flipped three cards from the deck, lining them up in the center of the table.

A four of hearts, a king of spades, and a six of hearts.

These were the "community cards."

In Texas Hold'em, you make hands of five using the cards in your hand and these community cards.

These hands were made according to the same rules as any other type of poker.

Well, between the king of diamonds in my hand and the king of spades on the table, I've got one pair, at least…

Might be a decent start.

"Okaaay. Bet time! That's *bet* with a *t*, not any naughty bedtime shenanigaaaaans."

"Quit it. You're up first this time. Hurry it up."

"Right, riiiiight. Well, I'm gonna go for iiiit."

Sorella put two brown chips down. Same value as before.

What should Masato do?

She's not betting the house here…and I have a pair… Might as well keep going.

He felt like he had a decent shot. "Call," he said.

Now there was 400,000 mum on the table.

The third round of betting was called the "turn."

"You only turn over one card heeeere. Don't screw it uuuup."

"Yeah, I know… Here goes."

Masato flipped one card from the deck, adding it to the community cards.

The fourth card was a seven of hearts.

Nice! I've got two pairs now!

He wanted to shout with joy, but he wasn't stupid enough to let Sorella know what he had, so he maintained his poker face. His hands were twitching a little, but he kept his cool.

Sorella watched him closely as she made her bet.

"Mmmm… I suppose this will doooo," she said, tossing another two brown coins. "Your turn, Masatooo. Or are you ready to fooold?"

"I can't leave this match now… Raise."

Raising meant increasing the amount bet, and this had to be double the current bet or more. It was an aggressive tactic.

Sorella's not betting big… I bet she's got nothing. But I've got two pairs!

Masato threw in an orange 250,000-mum chip.

"Ohhhh! Look who's feeling confideeent. Got yourself a good haaaand?"

"Maybe, maybe not… Your turn. What'll it be? Call or fold?"

"Weeeell... Maaaybe the next card will be a good one...so I'll caaaall."

Sorella removed her two brown chips and replaced them with an orange one.

Both bets were even, so it was time for the next round.

The current total stood at 900,000 mum.

The last round of betting was called the "river."

"This is the last one. What's it gonna be...?!"

Masato turned over one last card—a king of clubs.

He kept calm, not moving a muscle on his face. He sat back down and pumped his fist under the table.

On the table were a four of hearts, a king of spades, a six of hearts, a seven of hearts, and a king of clubs.

In his hand were a seven of spades and a king of diamonds.

He could make a hand of five from any of these seven cards. This gave him three kings and a pair of sevens—a full house.

I win.

A full house was pretty good hand in poker. Naturally, it couldn't compare to ridiculously unlikely hands like a royal straight flush. But it was plenty strong. You wouldn't often lose with one of these. He definitely wasn't about to.

Masato was certain of victory. He knew he had this in the bag.

"Whew... Time for the climax. Place your bet."

"Right, riiiight. I'll staaart...but instead, I think a check is in oooorder."

"Check" meant you were passing the right to make the first bet to the next player.

Since Sorella had checked, Masato would start the betting.

Now, how much should I bet...?

This was his fight to win, but that didn't mean he should raise the stakes immediately.

If Sorella sensed she was about to lose and folded, he'd still win, but all he'd get was what was already on the table.

If possible, he'd like to squeeze some more out of her and make off with a mountain of high-value chips.

But first, he had to bait her into it.

"...Bet," he said, putting all six brown chips he had left on the table.

A 300,000-mum bet.

"Quite a bit higher than befoooore. I guess I should do the saaame! Raaaaise!"

Sorella put out six brown chips, then added two orange ones.

An 800,000-mum bet.

Sorella was in. Good.

"Then I'll raise again."

Masato left the brown chips alone and added all nine of his orange chips.

A 2,500,000-mum bet—more than triple the previous one. Immediately after making it, he worried he was upping the stakes too fast.

"Wooow. Aren't you feistyyyy. I think I'll raise, toooo."

Sorella also put in her remaining seven orange chips and then added all ten of her gold chips at once.

A 7,550,000-mum bet.

She, too, was tripling the previous bet. Masato was getting a little nervous, but…

She's trying to scare me into folding… I'm sure of it!

The first to flinch lost. That's how these things worked. Masato had been through his share of tough fights, sword in hand, and he knew that only too well.

Then again, most of the time Mamako had done all the fighting…

Whatever.

"Now, Masatooo… What do you saaay?"

"Obviously… Raise!"

Masato threw in his ten gold chips, and not backing down at all, he threw in all his rainbow chips, too.

A 17,550,000-mum bet.

A big fight. One he was certain to win.

"Hoh-hooooh. You mean busineeeeess… Heh-hehhh… Then I guess I'll caaall."

Sorella put in ten rainbow chips, matching his bet. Including the previous rounds…

…the total amount on the table was 36,000,000 mum.

A terrifying amount of money and a huge mountain of chips.

All Masato's attention was on the two hands about to be revealed.

This moment of the game was called the "showdown."

"Since you were all aggressive and raised last, you show fiiiirst."

"Okay, sure. I've got…a full house."

Masato was certain he'd won.

But Sorella's countenance didn't change at all. Her eyes still looked sleepy, her manner languid, her voice soft. "Mwa-ha-haaa… Masatooo… Such a shaaame."

Sorella's hand was a three of hearts and a five of hearts.

Combined with the four, six, and seven of hearts in the community cards, she had a three, four, five, six, and seven of the same suit—a straight flush.

Which beat a full house.

Masato lost.

"…"

He found himself at a loss for words. He couldn't even breathe. What had just transpired was perfectly clear, and yet he couldn't understand it.

Sorella seemed to be thoroughly enjoying the sight of him frozen to the spot.

"Mwa-ha-haaa," she drawled. "You looooooose."

"N-no way… Hold up! Wait just a second!"

"The results wait for no maaaan… I captured Porta in mere moooo-ments, and Wise and Medhi tried to win her baaack, but they both loooost. And now you tried to get all three baaack, but you lost to me, toooo. That's how it goooooes."

The hero Masato had gone up against one of the Four Heavenly Kings of the Libere Rebellion with his companions' futures on the line and lost.

BAD END

And that was just…unacceptable.

Masato slapped the daze off his face, trying to reset his mind.

He wasn't going to let it end here. This wasn't over.

"Not yet! I haven't lost yet!"

"No, nooo… The game is already—"

"You said our battle would be decided by gambling in this casino. Well, I'm not finished yet. I still have chips left!"

"That's called being a sore looooser. But okaaaay. You're riiiight… Go ahead and struggle, it's all pooointless. Pffft."

"Pointless or not, you're damn right I'm gonna struggle! That's what a hero does!"

Masato still had a case of low-value chips. Low value, but the total was still worth 163,000 mum.

Clutching tightly to this sliver of hope, Masato left the table.

He headed for the slot corner.

"Gotta start by increasing the chips I have left!"

Slot machines had two types: flat tops that made frequent low payments and progressive machines that had low odds of scoring a huge jackpot.

If he wanted to increase his stake, common sense dictated he should go for the flat tops. He had enough experience with online games to know that much.

"Not like I'm afraid to take a risk! But I can't afford to lose today. Gotta play it safe and slowly build things up! That's important!"

Talking himself into it with some convincing excuses, Masato poured his chips into a video slot machine.

Placing the minimum bet on all lines he could, he pressed the AUTO SPIN button, letting it turn the reels automatically. Now he just had to wait for a hit…

Then…

"Sheesh! Gotta build up my stake on the stupid slot machines. My fate will be decided here! I'm putting it all on the line!"

A woman sat down on Masato's left and began pouring chips into the machine. She sounded like she'd been on a losing streak and was getting rather worked up about it.

Wait.

"…Yo."

"…Hmm?"

The girl next to him had a wild ponytail and a long black coat slung over her shoulders.

It was one of the Four Heavenly Kings of the Libere Rebellion— Anti-Mom Amante, she who rejects the concept of mothers.

Masato and Amante stared at each other for a long time, then gasped and tried to take up combat stances... But neither one was about to abandon their seats, so they wound up half standing, clutching their slot machine, and glaring at each other.

"You... What are you doing here?!"

"I'm not gonna answer that! Not this time! No reason I should tell you that I came to help another one of the Four Heavenly Kings, Sorella, in her battle against Mamako Oosuki, but she laaanguidly turned me down!"

"Man, it's such a help how you always explain these things! ...So Sorella wasn't kidding about being one of the Four Heavenly Kings, huh?"

"I tooold yoooou. You didn't belieeeve meeee? So meeean. Waaah, waaah."

Speak of the devil. Sorella came walking laaaanguidly over to them and sat down next to Masato.

Sorella on his right, Amante on his left, a slot machine before him. Two of the Four Heavenly Kings and a hero, all in a row.

...*Sheesh, this is...a really bizarre sight...*

Like he was starting to lose track of what *enemy* even meant.

Still.

"*Gasp...* Y-y'know...I'm starting to think I might be in real danger here... Like mortal danger..."

"Mwa-ha-haa. Maaaaybe. You might get killed at any seeeecond..."

"As if. I mean, Sorella's using her skill. And the effect of it means everyone in the casino's stats are at rock bottom. Even if I were to attack Masato Oosuki right now, I'd do, like, zero damage to him. Wouldn't even be worth calling a fight."

"She's got a skill like that? ...Oh, so was that why you looked like you were glowing earlier—?"

"Geeeez! You and your loose liiiips! Amante, you really are the duuuumbest! You're such a peeeest! Please just go awaaay!"

"Oh, I will! You don't even have to tell me! ...You're the worst, you know that?"

Apparently, Amante had just run out of chips. Furious, she punched the video slot machine as hard as she could.

She was strong enough to defeat a boss designed for guilds to fight, and yet the machine simply rocked slightly, remaining unharmed. Clearly, her stats really were at rock bottom.

"I've got that passive skill that reflects all attacks, and I thought I might be able to reflect Sorella's skill with that... But I guess I can't reflect anything that doesn't have a hitbox. And if she's lowered your Luck stat, there's no way you're ever gonna win gambling against her. So I'm calling it a day."

"You're quitting because you keep losing? Incredible."

"So duuumb. Also, you can't reflect debt, eeeeither. Make sure you paaay."

"Debt? ...Heh, I can handle that..."

Amante sneered confidently, snorted, and yelled, "Escape is victory!" She burst into a run. "Catch her, pleeease." """Yes, ma'am!"""" An army of black suits gave chase.

So.

While that was happening, the reels on Masato's slot machine ground to a halt.

This was a flat-top machine, and it should be throwing out regular small wins, but he'd gone this entire time without lining up a single set of images. It had eaten all his chips, leaving him with nothing.

But Masato was still perfectly calm.

"...Can I ask you something, manager?"

"Noooo. At least, if you're going to accuse me of cheating, then you'd better come armed with prooooof. Clear, visible prooooof. Or a confeeeession. If you can't do either, I'm in the cleeear. Mwa-haaa."

"*Tch*, that's a load of crap and you know it. A skill that tanks our stats is invisible, so I can't prove it."

"Mwa-ha-haaaa. Soooo? Now that you're flat broke, Masatoooo, that means I've defeated youuuuu... Now all I have to do is go beat Mamakooooo, and victory is miiiine."

"...You, beat Mom?"

"That's riiiight. Of course, in gambliiiing. I'll win so eeeeasily. Skills don't count as cheating or anythiiiing. But Mamako's going to lose right here in my casiiiiino. So saaad."

Such confidence.

Masato just shook his head and let out a long sigh.

"Mom's gonna lose, is she? ...*Sigh*... Have you looked behind you lately?"

"Mmmm? Whyyyy?"

Sorella slooowly turned around.

Mamako was sitting at a slot machine nearby.

"Oh no! Oh my goodness! I don't know what to do! They just keep coming out!"

High-value chips were spewing out of the slot machine, burying her lap.

Sorella's sleepy eyes shot wide open. She blinked rapidly, and her jaw nearly dislocated with surprise.

"Huh—? ...Whaaaaaa—?! What is thiiiiiiiiiiiiiiiiiiiiiis?!"

"Nicely done, Mom."

"M-Ma-kun! Mommy's in trouble! The chips won't stop coming out! Did I break the slot machine?!"

"No, not at all. Kinda the opposite..."

Mamako looked seriously at risk of being buried under chips, so he went over and helped pull her out.

He looked at the screen, and sure enough, the word JACKPOT was dancing across it.

Masato just shook his head, but Sorella staggered over, completely at a loss.

"But howwww?! How did you get a jackpoooot?!"

"Sorry. That's just what she does... You may have your skill active or whatever, but...that stuff's useless against her."

"Th-that's not possibleeee! Not that I was cheatiiiiing, but my skill is the strongest debuff effect in the entire woooorld! It tanks all your skills and luuuuck, so even Mamako is doomed to faaaail! ...A-anyway, Mamako, come with meeee!"

"O-oh, okay..."

Sorella grabbed Mamako's arm and dragged her away.

They made a beeline for the center of the casino hall, in front of the giant keno machine.

Keno worked a lot like bingo. You placed bets on several numbers from one to eighty, and the more numbers that matched what the machine picked, the more you won, a very simplistic game.

Sorella gave Mamako a quick rundown and thrust a betting slip into her hand.

"All right, Mamako, pick ten numbers—go oooon! We'll get that machine spinniiiing! And with your luck depleted, you'll lose, and I'll be deliiiighted!"

"Wow, you're just saying that to her face..."

"I just have to pick ten numbers between one and eighty? That's easy! ...Now, then..."

The numbers Mamako marked off were as follows:

Four, twenty-five, fifteen, one, seventy-two, sixty-five, twenty-six, five, thirty-six, and seventy-five.

Ten in all.

"Uh, Mom, any reason why you went with those?"

"Well, they're your birthday, and then your age, and then your height and weight, and then your shoe size, and then your body temperature and heart rate from yesterday when you were learning how to be spoiled."

"Okay, stop; that's enough. I'm already mortified... And when did you take my temperature and pulse anyway?"

"I can tell that much just by touching you! I'm a mother, after all. Hee-hee."

"R-right... Love is a terrifying thing sometimes..."

"Who caaares! Hit that buttonnn!"

The balls began whirling in the giant flask, passing down tubes and appearing in front of them one at a time. The first to pop out was...

...a ball with a *4* written on it.

"Oh my! I've already got one!"

"Yep. I can see where this is going."

"I-it's not over yetttt! You'll miss the next oooone! I'm sure of iiiit!"

Delighted, dejected, and desperate. Three very different reactions, but the machine kept on spitting out balls.

The *4* was followed by a *25*, then a *15*, then a *1*... You get the point.

When all ten numbers were out, the final results came to:

Four, twenty-five, fifteen, one, seventy-two, sixty-five, twenty-six, five, thirty-six, and seventy-five.

The end.

"Look! Look, Ma-kun! I got them all right!"

"Yep. I had a feeling you would. So…"

"Ngggggggghhh?! I-I'm not done yetttt! This isn't ooover!"

The sore loser grabbed Mamako's arm and pulled her over to the Texas Hold'em table where Masato and Sorella had played their fateful game.

"There's a special rule todaaay. People who win at kenoooo…get to bet all their chips heeeere, and if they win, they get them all baaack! Mamako haaaas… Hmm… Fifty million in aaaall, it seeeeems? That's pleeeenty!"

"Yo, hang on! That's not how this works! She's got all the chips she started with, plus she hit the jackpot at the slot machine! She's got way more than that!"

"The manager has spoooken! No arguiiiing! Do as I say or I won't let you cash iiiin!"

"Now you're just making stuff up!"

"But if we don't win, we can't get everyone back, right? We might as well try."

"Wait, Mom! Don't sit down!"

"She took a seeeeat! That means she agrees to participaaate! If you don't understand, just ask Masatooo! The forced bet is fifty million! Let's goooo!"

Bunny Girls were scurrying around with chips, and Sorella, looking quite beside herself, started dealing.

Two cards were dealt to each, and since the first round of betting, the pre-flop, was already accounted for, they went straight to the second round, the flop.

"All right, three for the community caaaards! Here we goooo!"

"Uh, hey! She hasn't even checked her hand!"

The cards on the table were a ten of hearts, a king of hearts, and an ace of hearts.

"Hey, Ma-kun, what should Mommy do?"

"W-well, first, check your hand! And make sure she can't see it—carefully!"

"Got it. Carefully..." *Peek.*

Mamako looked at the two cards in her hand. Masato peeked as well, stressing it.

A queen of hearts and a jack of hearts. Like a kindly queen and her son.

So, uh. Wow.

Masato wasn't even surprised. He just sighed as if this had been foreordained.

"You've done it again... That much hasn't changed..."

"Hey, Ma-kun, if I combined this with the three on the table, that would be a royal stress, right?"

"Whoever heard of such high-class stress? That's not even what that hand's called. And you're supposed to keep it a secret, remember?"

"Ooooh, what's thiiiis? You have a royal straight fluuuush? ...Woooow, pleeease, there's no waaay. You can't scare me that eeeasy."

"We're not— No, I don't even care anymore... We start the betting from this round, right? We can pay for the chips later and use as many as we want, so...fifty million."

The Bunny Girls put fifty rainbow chips on the table for him.

Sorella opened her eyes wide, blinking.

"U-ummm... You want to keep plaaaying? I-I'm not falling for such an obvious bluff, you knoooow. Fine, I'll caaaaaall. The next round is the tuuurn!"

"The fourth card... A three of clovers!"

"They're called 'clubs,' Mom. Doesn't matter what else comes out. Time to bet. Same amount again."

"Y-you're still goiiiing?! B-b-b-but I'm not gonna drop oooout! Caaaall! The last round of bets, the riverrrr!"

"The fifth card is the eight of spades!"

"Bet. Same again."

"F-fiiiine! I'll take you oooon! And I'll raaaaise! Double it! One hundred million!"

"Then we'll raise, too. Double again! Two hundred million!"

"Errrkkk?! Th-th-th...th-then...I'll raise by two and a half! Five hundred million!"

"Raise! Double it to one billion!"

"Heeeeeeyyyyy! I—I can't go further... I have to call...!"

The raise battle had the entire table buried in rainbow chips.

With a grand total of 2,300,000,000 mum on the line, it was time for the showdown.

After that aggressive betting, Masato and Mamako revealed their hand. The queen of hearts turned over. Followed by the jack...

"PAAAAAAAAAUSE!!" Sorella shrieked, her expression far too tragic. Was she trying to pause the game? That's what it sounded like. He knew how she felt.

"You can't pause this..."

"W-w-we can if I say we doooo! I get one pause per maaaatch! I'm the manager, and I say it's soooo! It's a special ruuule!"

"There you go, making stuff up again."

"Th-thennnn...we leave all the chips on the taaaable, and we deal new cards and do the showdown with thooose! Okay, dealiiiing!"

Sorella hastily swept up all the cards, shuffled for a really long time, said a prayer, and then dealt to their hands.

Sorella immediately laid the five community cards:

Ten of hearts, king of hearts, ace of hearts, three of clubs, and an eight of spades.

The exact same cards as before.

Sorella's blinking was almost strobe-like.

"Wh-what the...? Hmmm? W-wow, that's...a coincideeeence! B-but there's no way you got a royal straight flush twice in a roooow!"

"Yep. That's completely out of the realm of possibility... But there's just one thing I'd like to say."

"Wh-what's thaaat?"

"My mom's the master of the two-hit attack."

Sorella flinched once, then froze.

Meanwhile, Mamako quietly checked her cards: a queen of hearts and a jack of hearts.

At the time, nobody noticed—not Sorella, not Masato, not Mamako.

But Mamako had a skill active. And this skill was called **A Mother's Spoiling.**

This was a unique skill that she had acquired the day before, after spending a blissful mother-child date with Masato and spoiling him to her heart's content. The spoil power within her influenced her surroundings, spoiling the rules of games and the skills others used on her.

And what happened as a result…need not be said.

The unsettling battle was over, and it was time to settle up.

"Manager. This is the final summation. For your approval."

"A one-billion-one-hundred-million-mum loan to Mamako…and we end up paying one billion two hundred million mum… I can't believe it… I can't… Ugh…"

Sorella handed the paper back to the elderly assistant manager, a stricken look on her face. Then she fell over, foaming at the mouth, and was carried out on a stretcher. Poor thing.

With Sorella KO'd, the assistant manager bowed deeply.

"The amount owed to Mamako Oosuki is extremely high and thus requires the manager's approval. But as the manager is out of commission…I'm afraid payment and prize exchanges will have to be tomorrow or later."

"You can't do anything…? We'd really like to get our party members back…"

"Hmm… If you can't let us claim them today, can we at least ask that you make sure nobody else can claim them? Is that possible?" asked Mamako.

"Understood. I do apologize for the delay. Your request is entirely reasonable. The casino will be closing immediately. Thank you for coming."

It wasn't like they'd won the battle and lost the war…

…but they would have to wait at least a day to claim their companions.

Meanwhile, in the prize warehouse in the staff dorm:

"Ughhh! The heck? Why do we have to clean?!" moaned Wise.

"Cleaning is just an excuse. They just wanted to get us away from those two, so we don't give them any extra information," replied Medhi.

"I'm not super-happy about it, either, but this is our job, so we'd better get this place clean!" Porta added.

Grumbling, the three girls dutifully plunged themselves into work. Still dressed as Bunny Girls, they took rags in their hands and began carefully wiping down the prizes.

Then there was a knock on the door, and several men in black came in, carrying a coffin.

"Hard at work, girls? We've brought that new prize. Can you take it from here?"

"Yep, got it! Thanks for carrying it all this way! ...So anyway."

"It's definitely her inside, right?" asked Medhi.

"Oh! I wanted to claim this coffin, but can I do that now?" inquired Porta.

"Huh? Uh, sure," one of the men replied. "They said staff could claim it, so go ahead. You'll need a one-mum chip to claim it, but..."

"Okay! I have one!"

Porta pulled out the front of her leotard, stuck her hand in, and pulled out a single white chip. A chip warmed by the chest of a twelve-year-old girl.

"Here you go!"

"I will treasure this forever and use a different chip to complete the exchange."

The man in black pulled out a handkerchief and carefully wrapped it around the chip. "Gimme that!" "Can I have a sniff?" "Stop that!" He left, arguing with the others. Such merry guards.

Anyway. The three girls gathered around the coffin, thinking.

"It's one thing to accept the thing, but what now?"

"Neither Wise nor I can use magic...and we can't take items out of Porta's bag...so I guess we should just keep this in our room?"

"I think that's all we can do! As soon as we're done cleaning, we should carry it... Huh? There's something sticking out!"

Porta leaned over and pulled out a piece of paper stuck under the coffin lid:

A Plea for the Recovery of Valuables

It was a flyer, like one asking for donations to a fund-raiser at a local elementary school. There were drawings of flowers and animals around it, of a quality one could only call cute if they were being extremely polite.

The actual body of the text, like the title implied, was a request to recover a valuable item. No deadline given.

And the item could be found in the casino basement.

"Recover a valuable item from the basement? What valuable item? Does this casino even have a basement? I don't remember seeing any stairs leading down. What do you think, Medhi?"

"I'm as confused as you are... But I wonder if this information is—?"

Before Medhi could finish her sentence, the coffin started rattling. "Eeek?!" "Wh-what the—?!" "Wow! It's going wild!" It certainly seemed to want to say *something*.

Medhi took the hint and rephrased.

"Um, uh... Maybe this infooormation was intended for us. Something she intended to infooorm us about?"

"Oh, I guess that's possible. She planned to call us here like always, but before she did, another bug killed her... And the casino flyer was..."

"I think we can safely assume that was sent by the manager, Sorella. Either way, this infooormation is clearly the real one."

"You want us to recover this valuable?! Should we?!" Porta asked the coffin. There was no reply.

Apparently, it would be a while before they could get detailed infooormation out of the coffin lady.

CHUTES AND MOTHERS

2

⑫ **MOMMY IS COOKING! ♪ ROLL THE DIE AND WAIT UNTIL YOU ROLL A ONE.**

⑪ **"DID I LOCK UP...?" GO BACK FOUR SPACES TO CHECK.**

⑥ **JOIN MOMMY! ADVANCE TO THE SPACE SHE'S ON!**

⑤ **GET A HUG FROM MOMMY!**

START HERE!

Masato | Mamako
Wise | Medhi

GOAL! GOOD JOB.

⑩ **HELP WITH HOUSEWORK! TWENTY PUSH-UPS FOR ALL THAT HARD LABOR.**

⑦ **NAP WITH MOMMY. REST A TURN.**

④ **YOU FORGOT YOUR WALLET! GO BACK TO START.**

① **SAY GOOD-BYE TO MOMMY! "SEE YOU LATER!"**

Porta

※If you don't stop exactly on the goal, go back however many you have left over.

⑨ **SAY SOMETHING AS IF YOU WERE MOMMY.**

⑧ **AN ALLOWANCE FROM MOMMY! OBTAIN 1,000,000 MUM!**

③ **GET A LECTURE FROM MOMMY. SIT ON YOUR KNEES!**

② **GO ON A WALK WITH MOMMY. ADVANCE FOUR SPACES.**

Mommy got...a five! Okay, Ma-kun, give Mommy a hug! Hee-hee!

I'm not your mom, though, am I?!

Second round. I got...a three...

Wise, time to get on your knees. Hurry now!

It says to *sit* on my knees, not grovel! Besides, you also got a three, Medhi!

I rolled a one again! ...Advance one space, then four more... That's the sixth space, so now I move to where Mama is!

Then I get to hug you, Porta!

Anything but a five or a six... Anything but those... A six! Arghhhh!!

Chapter 3 Three Bunny Girls and Two Bunny Moms Make a Full House! I'm So Not Thrilled!

The next day arrived.

Masato and Mamako entered the casino the moment it opened for business with one goal in mind. They headed straight for the exchange counter to claim their prizes.

After a long wait:

"Masato! Mama! Good morning!"

"Mornin'! We've been waiting for you guys!"

"Good morning! We're going to be free at last! I can hold my head... No, my ears high once more!"

Leading the pack was Bunny Porta, followed by Bunny Wise and Bunny Medhi close behind. The three of them came happily running over.

They were dancing with joy, excitedly hopping around, swaying...

"Hey! Masato! What are you staring at? Pervert."

"Don't call me that! I was looking at your bunny ears! Besides, any swaying your boobs might do is undetectable to the human eye."

"Okay, got it—time to kick your ass."

"I personally feel I was subjected to an inappropriate gaze. Therefore, Masato, I demand compensation. One hundred fifty million mum will suffice."

"I knew you'd say that, Medhi, and that's why I didn't look. Also, stop trying to squeeze money out of your friends."

Having greeted one another and received a stomp on the foot from Wise, Masato thought to himself:

They seem fine... Glad to see them in good spirits.

However, he did not admit to this relief out loud. He felt it was best left secret.

Meanwhile, Porta had sadly thrown her arms around Mamako instead.

"Mama! I missed you sooo much!"

"Aw, such a spoiled little girl. Hee-hee."

"Eep! Sorry! I got carried away..."

"That's okay. I love spoiling you. I missed having you around, too, Porta. But it's okay now. We're about to get you back."

Then they began the final paperwork. Mamako and the staff at the exchange counter set to work.

He left it in her hands.

"Oh, Wise, Medhi, got a sec?"

Somewhat reluctant, he gathered them around.

He figured he'd better be up front about this so there were no hard feelings later.

"This is just my opinion, but I was thinking we should prioritize getting Porta back. Is that cool?"

"No, that's totally fine. I mean, Porta was only here in the first place because Medhi tricked her into it. And Medhi forced her to cheat and use her skill, too. Porta's the real victim here."

"And you agreed to all of it, Wise. You're an accomplice. Equally guilty... But there's no real point in arguing that here. Masato, you don't need to worry about us."

"That's right! Doesn't matter who's first and who's last. Crap like that's not gonna change anything between us, I promise."

"O-okay... Guess I was worried about nothing."

"You were. So go on, Masato; say it'll be me you choose to claim along with Porta."

"Wha—? Medhi, what the heck? I'm clearly second in line here."

Things sure got awkward fast. Wise glared, Medhi smiled, and neither said another word. Each refused to believe what the other had said.

Yeah.

"Uh... Let's all try to stay calm here... Mom won one billion two hundred million mum, and if we use one billion of that to claim Porta..."

"There's two hundred million mum left! I'm only one hundred million, so you can easily claim me," said Wise.

"Or use one hundred fifty million to claim me."

"Right… But, uh, first…"

Masato held out an invoice.

"What the…? Two hundred million mum for refreshments?"

"They gave this to us at the exchange counter… It's your, uh, room service bill. We've gotta pay this off first."

"Huh? W-wait… Two hundred million for room service?!"

"We did ask for some snacks and drinks, but…nothing worth anything that much!"

"I'm pretty sure this is just sour grapes on Sorella's part. But it does mean we're outta dough. So…"

Masato left the last words hanging. The two girls turned to each other.

"Medhi! I'm so glad you're my friend!" *Beam.*

"I agree! We get along so well!" *Beam.*

All smiles, the two girls left behind renewed their vows of friendship. Arm-in-arm, they surreptitiously gave each other elbow jabs. *Fraternité!*

Masato left them to it. "You're not innocent, either, Masato." "You ate those macarons, after all." "Those were crazy expensive!" Masato received a few elbow jabs as well.

Meanwhile, Mamako and Porta came back from the exchange counter.

"Thanks for waiting! We've finished Porta's paperwork."

"I'm free again! Look at my stats!"

Porta popped up her stat screen, showing it off.

Her job was listed as Traveling Merchant again. She was still dressed as a Bunny Girl and was hopping around merrily, but she was back to normal.

"I can access the party storage again! I can do Item Creation! I can be useful!"

"Wonderful! Such a relief."

"The items and equipment are important, but more than anything, Porta's the one who keeps our party going… She plays a vital role in diverting some of Mom's attention from me. I'm so glad to have you back, Porta… All right, so…"

Now that she was back…

"Let's go have an adventure!"

"Okay! I'll follow you anywhere!"

"Let's go find us a nice safe town without any dangerous casinos."

The three of them walked merrily away.

"......"

Wise and Medhi said nothing, their eyes as dead as those of dolls thrown in a dumpster. It was genuinely terrifying. "W-we're kidding, I swear!" "It was a joke!" "It was!" Just some light humor. They didn't mean it!

"U-um, we'll figure out how to get the two of you back before the day is over. Don't worry! Right, Mom?"

"Of course! Wise and Medhi are as much a part of this party as you and Porta. We would never abandon them!"

"I'll help in any way I can without getting in trouble again!"

"Thanks, Mamako, Porta. We need the help...but we'll put in the effort, too. We're not gonna end up like Masato, sitting helplessly in Mamako's shadow."

"I'll do what I can, too. We only need one party member as spineless as Masato, pathetically relying on Mamako to do everything. Unlike him, I'm not a wimp."

"Argh... You weren't even there... You aren't actually wrong, though..."

"Anyway, it's time we got back to work."

"Mamako, Porta, we'll say good-bye for now."

Wise gave Mamako and Porta a hug and gave Masato a frosty glare. Medhi gave Mamako and Porta a hug and shot a pasted-on smile in Masato's direction. "Such discrimination..." Masato briefly but genuinely considered leaving them here.

"Oh, duh! Porta, you can use revival items now, right?" Wise asked.

"That's true. Can you take care of that coffin?" added Medhi.

"Okay! Leave it to me! I'll bring her back to life and get tons of infooormation out of her!"

"Infooormation from a coffin...?"

"Oh, I see; you already claimed that? Then before we start earning money, we'd better take care of her... I wonder what infooormation she has."

Wise and Medhi left to handle their Bunny Girl work. Masato, Mamako, and Porta went to see you-know-who.

Each group had their own tasks to handle.

Meanwhile, in the manager's office:

"Reporting. Procedures for exchanging Porta have been completed."

"Arghhhh… She was our captiiiive! And Mamako Oosuki just snatched her awaaay. I am so upsetttt. Waaah, wahhh."

Sorella collapsed on her desk, kicking her arms and legs like a sulky toddler. The extra years she had on Masato didn't seem to mean much…

But it was too late to complain. She knew that well enough.

As if trying to drive the gloom away, Sorella slapped her desk really hard and stood up.

"Hng. Okaaay. Thanks for the repoooort… Then I'm gonna activate my skiiiill. The customers' luck stats will go up, so you go and control the win rates on the floooor."

"You're activating your skill? …If you do that, they'll easily get the other two back…"

"Who cares if they doooo? I only wanted Portaaaa… So unfaaaair. Anywaaaay. If they start poking around in the baaaasement, that will be much woooorse… I'll leave the casino itself to youuu, then. All rights are youuuurs. Enjooooy."

"Understood. I shall do as you ask."

Not batting an eye at her cavalier attitude, the assistant manager bowed low.

Sorella sighed dramatically and settled back into her favorite executive chair.

"Whewww… Everything suuucks. But whateeeever. Unlike Dumbmante, I don't caaare if I fight Mamako Oosuki or noooot… My focus is on the Rebellion's plaaaans… If the experiments here succeeeeed… Mwa-ha-haaa…"

She was referring to the Libere Rebellion, a group fighting against the concept of parents. As one of their leaders, Sorella prioritized the goals of the group over her personal successes.

If their ongoing experiments were completed without issue, the Rebellion would win.

So the fact that Mamako had easily won, despite Sorella's skill, and taken Porta back didn't really matter.

"Rrrghhhh! I'm so maaaad!" *Slap, slap, slap, slap.*

Her hair disheveled, Sorella beat her desk like a drum. She wasn't the type to stifle her emotions.

"Arghhhhh! Right, that does iiit! I'm gonna go take it out on those other awful moooothers! Everything's all set for me to have a little fuuun!"

Sorella took some papers out of a desk drawer.

They were filled with data about the residents of Yomamaburg, with particular details on the families' structures.

For instance, which ones were mothers and whose children were whose. She went over this information with evident malice.

"Mwa-ha-haaaa… Foolish, useless traaaash. The casino is open for all you awful mooothers. Mwa-ha-haaa!"

Sorella jumped to her feet and laaanguidly left the manager's office.

Masato, Mamako, and Porta had left the shop and entered the staff dorm.

As they walked down the hall, Masato read over the flyer with A PLEA FOR THE RECOVERY OF VALUABLES written on it.

"So this flyer was sticking out of the coffin, and it says… Hmm…"

"Wise and Medhi think this is our real mission! The casino flyer was sent by Sorella!"

"She's admitted to it, so that part's definitely true. Well, regardless, we were going to end up here anyway."

"Casino flyer? Ma-kun, what are you—?"

"Oh… There was this flyer, and that's why we ended up forming a secret plan… I'll explain later once this mess is all cleaned up. This is our priority now!"

They entered the room the girls had slept in.

Yep. Definitely more a suite than a room. The place was filled with sweet scents and piles of insanely expensive room service snacks and drinks.

"Where is she?"

"We felt bad leaving her on the floor, so she's on a bed! Over here!"

Porta led them into one of the bedrooms.

There was a coffin lying on top of one of the queen-sized beds. "I'll bring her back!" Porta pulled a fist-sized orb out of her shoulder bag, placed it on the coffin...and it turned to mist, revealing the mysterious nun within. Definitely Shiraaase.

Shiraaase sat up and bowed, with her usual implacable expression.

"Why, hello, everyone. I am so grateful you've brought me back to life once more. I can infooorm you that I am the Shiraaase you know and love."

"That's an awfully strong turn of phrase."

"Oh, don't be that way. I am your supervisor, and we've become so close I almost count as a member of your party... Oh? Where are Wise and Medhi?"

"Yeah... It's a long story..."

"They've become Bunny Girls and are working at the casino!"

"I see. As long as we know where they are, let's call it good... Anyway, now that we've met, I must provide you with some special infooormation. As my name is Shiraaase."

Shiraaase turned her gaze toward the flyer in Masato's hand.

"I see you have already acquired the request I was going to make."

"I guess...you want us to recover a valuable item from the casino basement?"

"What is this valuable item, Ms. Shiraaase?" asked Porta.

"Some sort of treasure...?" wondered Mamako.

"Indeed. Think of it as a legendary secret if you like. After all, it is an item with the hidden power to control everyone in the world."

"Control everyone?" Masato muttered in disbelief. "That's...dramatic."

"It's the truth," Shiraaase said, dead serious. "The name of the item you are to recover is *Alzare*."

"Alzare? Weird name."

"Alzare is actually a program designed to set NPC thought and action patterns. Since using the program allows you to raise the characters like your own children, we took the name from the word for 'raise' in a certain language."

"An NPC setting program? If that's our goal, then...the implications..."

"Naturally, you have concerns. This is data vital to the creation of a game world and not anything ever intended to be found within the world itself. And yet...someone extracted this program somehow and turned it into an item. Or perhaps not someone—there may be a group responsible for this."

"A group... Oh, I see..."

The name Libere Rebellion sprang to mind.

"Yeah... Come to think of it, there were these brainwashed NPCs attacking their moms last time... Was that...?"

"The jewel of darkness recovered during this previous incident did possess that functionality. Fearing that the setting program had somehow been copied, we investigated for anything like that and discovered that the program itself had been stolen out from under our very noses."

"...No offense, but does operations understand the concept of security?"

"Our security against external threats is state of the art. However, we can do little to prevent internal malfeasance."

"Uh...internal?"

"Oh no, pretend you didn't hear that. The matter is still under investigation, so I'm unable to share the details at this time. I do beg your pardon."

It sounded like the investigation had made some headway, at least, but... "Um, Shiraaase—" "If you ask any further questions, I'll be forced to strip." She began hiking up the hem of her skirt. "U-understood! We won't ask!" The threat of a woman's flesh was extraordinary. No boy could possibly fight it.

Anyway.

"Operations investigated and discovered that Alzare appears to be in the basement of this casino. We would like you to recover this as soon as possible. We wish we could say 'before it is used for evil,' but..."

"Oh my! Has it already been used for evil?"

"Sounds like it has!"

"Hmm... The manager, Sorella, is one of the Libere Four Heavenly Kings... She's got a skill that tanks all stats, even luck, ensuring that nobody can win here, yet customers just keep flooding in... Definitely possible she's doing something underhanded. Still, that's not all she could be using it for."

"Oh-ho! You have already grasped the identity of the manager and her skill... You are a force to be reckoned with. In that case..." Shiraaase got off the bed and bowed her head low. "I do apologize for putting you through such tribulations every time, but once again...thanks much!"

"Wow. So cavalier."

"Since the game began we have given you one request after another. I imagined you were growing quite tired of earnest gratitude, so I attempted to change my manner. How was it?"

"We'd be delighted to help. Any request from you, Shiraaase."

"Yes! I'll help, too!"

"Mamako, Porta, I thank you. Thank you for making it so that it would be very awkward for Masato to refuse."

"Argh... Y-yeah, if Mom and Porta are in, there's no way I'm out... but I wish someone would at least ask my opinion first... Am I just along for the ride? This is no way to treat a hero. It never hurts to ask, y'know..."

No one cared.

But there was one point Masato was determined to make.

"Oh, right. I don't mind helping you out, Shiraaase, but what about Wise and Medhi? They're working at the casino to pay off their debts, so we've gotta win enough to buy them back."

"Oh, that's right! Mommy completely forgot!"

"True! We have to do our best at this casino!"

"Is that where they are? Hmm... However, I don't think you need concern yourselves."

"Is that so?"

"I'm afraid I can't share the details, but we've got an insider working this facility. They're quite reliable and will take care of the two of them. I'd like you three to focus on Alzare."

"Hmm... Well, if you say so..."

"Yes! Ma-kun, let's help Shiraaase!"

"I agree! I'll help!"

"Thank you very much. Let us begin preparations."

*   *   *

Meanwhile, in the casino hall, Wise was working hard.

"Here, I brought you a drink. See, now you gotta pay for it in chips. Don't be stingy; fork over all ya got."

"You're demanding chips before you even give me the drink? You're awfully aggressive for a Bunny Girl...but sure, why not. I'm on a winning streak. Here!"

"Ooh! Ten thousand? How generous! Thank you, thank you... Then I'll bring you a refill, so make sure you win enough for the next tip! Ta!"

"Um... I didn't ask for a refill..."

Medhi was working equally hard.

"Sir, may I bother you for a moment? I just want to check the contents of your pockets."

"Huh? There's nothing in my pocket... Huh?! Why are there cards in there? I—I didn't do that! I'm innocent! I'm not trying to cheat!!"

"It's certainly possible someone else planted these here, but now that I have accidentally uncovered this suspicious behavior, your life as you know it is over. My condolences."

"O-oh no... Wait, I've got it! I'll give you all the chips I just won! Pretend you saw nothing, okay? Please!"

"If you insist. But just this once! ...Heh-heh-heh."

Who put the card in that man's pocket? Let's hope it wasn't Medhi herself. It probably wasn't. Let's say so anyway.

Wise and Medhi met up, showing off piles of chips threatening to overflow their hands. Both were making bank, the grins on their faces nothing short of diabolical.

"Mwa-ha! Look at all this! I'm raking it in!"

"So it may seem, but mine are worth more than yours. I win."

"Yeah, yeah, if you say so. You owe more debt anyway... By the way, is it just me, or do you get the sense the customers are winning more today?"

"They are. I honestly don't see anyone losing."

"It's like the shop is secretly letting them win...which means..."

Wise scurried over to the slot corner, cradling her chips, and took a seat.

The machine she'd unconsciously selected was a flat top—lots of wins with smaller payouts. The perfect choice to increase the stake on hand. A stroke of luck.

"Riiight, then I'm gonna win a bunch, too! I'll just dump all my chips in here and go nuts!"

"Um, Wise... We're supposed to be working..."

"I know that! But we can't let this chance pass. Everyone oughta be able to win right now! Better than leaving it all up to Mamako, right?"

"True... I do want to get myself out of this one on my own if I can..."

"And we're not the only staff playing. See? Look there."

Wise pointed to a slot machine two seats over, where...

"I dunno what she was thinking, but Sorella activated her skill... This is my chance! The one shot I've got at recouping my losses! All my chips are going in!"

...another female staff member was muttering to herself as she poured chips into the machine.

This was no Bunny Girl. She was a tiger girl.

She had tiger ears on her head in place of the bunny ears... No, wait, those were just two bunches of her hair tied up. And her over-the-knee socks had a tiger print on them.

And that aggressive-looking ponytail and profile sure looked familiar...

Medhi twitched.

"W-Wise? I feel like I know that girl from somewhere..."

"Well, yeah, we're coworkers, so we're bound to have— ...Huh? Amante?"

"Who has the nerve to interrupt me when I'm— Huh?! What are you doing here?!"

Surprised, Amante tried to put some distance between them, but she'd just dumped all her chips into the slot machine and didn't want to leave it, so she wound up forced to stand her ground.

Wise was a little freaked out, too.

"Wh-why are *you* here...?"

"I came here to help Sorella, another one of the Four Heavenly Kings, but not only did she refuse my help, I ran up a huge debt here, which I'm trying to pay off. Not that I need to tell you any of that!"

"Oh, I—I see… Well, at least you're still explaining everything… That really helps us out."

"I've never once helped you! …Hmph. Whatever. I'm busy. I don't have time to deal with you. So I'll let you go this time. Scram."

"Um, uh… Then we'll do just—" Wise began to slowly edge away.

"Wise! She's our enemy! You can't just run away!"

"Wha—? Medhi! What am I supposed to do? She's crazy strong, remember? And since our jobs got switched to Bunny Girl, we can't use any magic! Our stats are all reduced to normal human levels! There's no way we can fight her!"

"So? It'll be a glorious death!"

"Then you do it! Look, you're trying to run away, too!"

Medhi had already retreated to the edge of the casino. Well done, Medhi.

Then…

"A wise decision. Go on, run away! That works out better for me anyway."

"…Huh? What do you mean?"

"I mean, I'm just like this Sage here. I got caught up in a bunch of debt and my job got changed. I'm basically a regular person now. My passive reflection skill doesn't even work. I'm ready to burst into tears and run away myself…but I'm not gonna admit to that out loud!" Amante said—out loud.

Well, that changed things.

Halfway through this, a sinister smile spread across Wise's face.

"Ohhh? You're in the same boat as us, then… In which case, this is our chance! We can take out one of the Four Heavenly Kings! Kick her ass!"

Wise was ready to throw down. She started cracking her knuckles.

A blue vein started throbbing on Amante's beautiful forehead, and she matched the intensity of Wise's glare. She wasn't one to back down from a fight.

"You kick *my* ass? Heh, that's a laugh… Fine! You're on! I'm always ready to turn one of Mamako Oosuki's party members into a corpse! …Although admittedly, I don't think I'm actually strong enough to do that right now!"

"We're fighting with girls' rules! This is a girl fight!"

"The cutest one wins!"

Wise and Amante instantly started posing!

Bunny Wise turned herself into the cutest Bunny Girl she possibly could, smiled from ear to ear, and blew a kiss! Smooch! ☆

Amante took full advantage of the whole big-cat thing and pulled off an arrogant but adorable cat pose! Meow! ☆

And off to the side:

"Line up, everyone! It's Bunny Girl versus tiger girl! Which one will win? Place your bets!"

"Oohhh... A contest to see who's cuter? That could be fun! Right, I bet a million on the Bunny Girl."

"Then I bet two million on the tiger girl! That's everything I've won today!"

"The winner will be whoever scores the most chips! Steal the victory for your side! Remember, these bets are essentially voting, so the chips you put in will not be returned to you."

This important final detail was delivered in a much quieter voice. The "bets" kept coming in.

And...

"...What spirited young ladies! Ha-ha-ha!"

...standing behind the two competitors was the elderly assistant manager, a warm smile on his face.

Back to the Alzare Search Team.

They hadn't even left the room yet, and Masato was already clutching his head.

"...Argh... I can't believe I have to look at this again..."

"Hee-hee! Bunny Mommy, hop!" *Wink!* ☆

Bunny Mamako returned. Her son's head hurt.

That alone would have been enough, but there was more.

"Masato, try to tear your eyes off Mamako long enough to evaluate me, bunny?"

"Uh, sure... I mean, Shiraaase..."

"I am no longer Shiraaase. I am Bunnyyyse, bunny."

"Uh, okay, if you say so… Do I really have to play along with this?"
Bunnyyyse stood proudly before Masato.

Bunny ears, high-cut leotard, fishnet tights, the whole Bunny Girl
thing. She was still in her midtwenties and in great shape, so she
looked pretty good, but…

…She actually had a child of her own, so that made her another
bunny mom.

"Heh-heh-heh… Masato, what do you think, bunny? Do you like me
as a Bunny Mom, bunny?"

"If you want a serious answer, it's way better than my own mom."

"Oh! A glowing review indeed, bunny. I'm quite surprised, bunny.
You approve of this bunny mom, then, bunny?"

"Compared to having your own mother dressed like that… Ha-ha…
I think I'd approve of just about anything else… Ha-ha…" He
crumbled.

"Clearly this is taking its toll on your state of mind, so I shall cease
teasing you, bunny."

"Um, um, Masato! Do I make a good Bunny Girl?!"

"You're supercute. Mega-cute. Your cuteness alone is my salvation."

"Th-thank you!"

The tiny Bunny Girl gave him a salute. Mm. He was healed.

At any rate, the girls were all wearing bunny costumes. And Masato's jacket was in Porta's storage, leaving him dressed like a fake dealer.

This was part of their plan.

"Now that we're all disguised as staff members, let's get going,
bunny," said Bunnyyyse. "This will be an infiltration, so everyone take
it seriously, bunny."

"You're the least serious one here!"

They left the room, heading down the hall.

This was an undercover mission. A serious, dignified one…

"Mamako, we have two bunny mothers, so we should team up."

"Oh, good idea! The two of us should hop along together!"

"Don't!! What're you even going to do, unleash a combo move that
instantly kills me?!"

"Come to think of it, Mamako… While we were changing earlier…"

"Oh, right! I was telling you all about how Ma-kun made me spoil him. And then Ma-kun asked to lay in my lap and have me read to him! Reading him a story with his head on my lap was ever so wonderful."

"I see. That is some next-level spoiling. And that's why you're over-flowing with power now?"

"It is. Even I'm scared of how amazing I feel! I'm sure it's because Ma-kun wanted me to spoil him. Hee-hee."

"I see, I see… So that's how you got that skill… Hmm…"

"I'm ready to die of shame over here!! Can we please change the subject?!"

It was impossible to stay serious with Bunnyyyse around. "Oh, you've stopped ending every sentence in 'bunny.'" "It just isn't the same if it doesn't roll back to the whole Shirase thing." "I suppose…" She was a woman of principles. Shirase-based principles. Then let's abandon the whole "Bunnyyyse" thing and just stick with "Shiraaase."

Then:

"Hold on. From this point forward, we actually do need to be serious."

Shiraaase stepped forward, peering around the corner. Then she waved them forward, and they peered around it, too.

There was a door ahead of them, heavily guarded by a number of black-suited bouncers.

Masato and Shiraaase took a step back, moving a safe distance away.

"…Is that…?"

"The stairs to the basement are believed to be inside that room. The merchant city of Yomamaburg is built on top of a legendary ancient city buried by history…"

"So there's old ruins under it? …Whoa, that's cool! I smell adventure! Sounds exciting!"

"By ancient, I mean the data was patched in quite recently, but…"

"Sure, it's a game! But the mood still matters, so respect it, will you? I don't know how many times I've asked you not to infooorm us about things like that…"

"I beg your pardon. I'll try to remember. Anyway, there's a rather large space beneath this casino. There are limited entry points, so it's ideal to hide things."

"And this Alzare is down there, huh?"

"Yes. However, as you can see, the entrance is heavily guarded, and we can't get anywhere close to it."

"So we've got to try and break through those guards somehow..."

"Let's try a frontal assault. Masato, can you help?"

"Oh, sure. Got it."

"Ma-kun, be careful!"

"Good luck!"

Mamako and Porta watched as Masato and Shiraaase moved forward. Pretending to be ordinary staff, they turned the corner...

"Halt."

...only for the guards to block them instantly. They seemed to be in a very bad mood, and their stares were merciless. Downright scary.

But Masato and Shiraaase kept their cool.

"H-hey, keep up the good work, guys. We're just ordinary staff members here!" said Masato.

"Understood. What brings you here?"

"We have business in that room. Can we get through?" asked Shiraaase.

"I'm afraid even staff members aren't allowed inside. Please turn back."

They were calmly turned away. The men in black didn't budge. Nothing to be done. "I—I see..." "Understood. Excuse us." They beat a retreat before anyone got suspicious.

Back around the corner, a safe distance away, they consulted Mamako and Porta.

"Goodness, looks like that was a bust."

"What should we do?!"

"These moments call for Mamako... Will you do the honors?" Shiraaase asked.

"Oh? What do you mean?"

Shiraaase whispered in Mamako's ear.

Mamako looked a little concerned, but in the end, she nodded.

"...Okay. I'll try it."

"Thank you so much. Let's go. All of us together this time."

It was unclear what plan they had, but Shiraaase seemed confident. Masato and Porta glanced at each other and decided to do as they were told.

When they approached the room again, the men in black blocked their path once more.

And then Mamako smiled.

"Guards, would you like to have some *fun* with me?"

What did she mean by "fun"? Masato, Porta, and the guards were all lost, their heads tilted in collective confusion.

Then Shiraaase stepped forward.

"Wow, you're all dense. A woman in a Bunny Girl outfit wants to have some *fun* with you. That only means one thing! Do we have to spell it out for you? ...Masato, a demonstration, if you would."

"Huh? Me?"

"And Porta, can you prepare a blindfold?"

"Oh, sure! Will cloth for Item Creation be enough?"

"That will do nicely. Please hand it to Masato."

Porta took a long, thin cloth out of her shoulder bag. "Here!" she said and handed it to Masato.

Masato took it but definitely didn't like where this was going.

"Um, Shiraaase... Why a blindfold? What are you trying to make me do?"

"This is part of our scheme to slip through the guards. That's all! Hurry. The ancient ruins are waiting for you! Your adventure is just beginning!"

"Ruins... Adventure... Argh, so tempting..."

He knew this wouldn't lead to anything good, but he wanted what was offered so badly that he grit his teeth and put the blindfold on.

"Such an obedient hero... Now, Mamako, please do what I mentioned earlier."

"Got it! I'm gonna give Ma-kun plenty of service!"

"Whoa, hold up. I don't like the sound of that."

"A demonstration! Guards, watch carefully."

With the blindfold on, Masato couldn't be sure how the guards reacted. He stood still, waiting...

Aaand then his head was pulled down, enveloped in something soft. Something warm and incredibly pleasant.

"Wh-what...is this...?"

"Okay, Ma-kun, let's go! Bunny Mommy's...Puff-Puff!"

"Wha—? Mmph!!"

Sandwiched between her breasts, one on each side—Puff-Puff—Masato's face felt warm, soft, compressed— Mmmppphhh!

Bunny Mommy's limited unique skill activated! A Mother's Puff-Puff!

The effect of it would make the recipient so comfortable that they would think they were ascending to heaven...

...but used against her own son, it was effectively a fatal blow. "Are you...trying to kill me...? ...Ugh..." "Oh no! Ma-kun?!" Getting a Puff-Puff from your mom was far too much for any teenage boy to handle. Trapped between Mamako's boobs, Masato went limp.

After a brief moment of silence for the fallen hero, Shiraaase turned to the guards.

"This ends our demonstration. What do you say?"

"A P-Puff-Puff?! You really offer that kind of service?!"

"And from a bunny mom... I heard the staff saying she showed up in the casino yesterday—you're offering us a Puff-Puff from *her*?!"

"Yes, as we have just demonstrated. So, gentlemen, would you like to have some *fun* with this bunny mama? Free of charge? Heh-heh-heh."

"W-wait! Everyone, calm down! ...You know what happens with Puff-Puffs! You get lured in and then end up with your face bouncing off some bodybuilder's pecs! Guaranteed!"

"Th-that's right! This is a trick! Nothing like this could ever really happen! Don't be fooled!"

The guards were certainly rattled, but they were just barely clinging to rationality.

But there was already a line forming in front of Mamako.

"You're all true to yourselves."

"Yes! Sorry for being men!"

"I don't care if we're being tricked! That's part of the Puff-Puff experience!"

"Well said... Now, Porta, blindfolds for everyone."

"Okay! Leave it to me!"

"Also, no touching the bunny mommy. We'll have to tie your hands behind your back to make sure nothing inappropriate happens. Understood?"

"Of course! Go ahead! Tie us up!"

"Oh, there's a room right here... If we were in that room, we could take our time and really enjoy this, but I'm afraid the door is locked..."

"I've got the room key! Use it, please!"

"I certainly will."

They had the key now. And the guards were blindfolded, their hands tied behind their backs.

They'd cleared the security checkpoint.

So Shiraaase, Mamako, Porta, and Masato (who'd managed to recover with the aid of some potions) slipped quietly through the door and locked it from the inside.

The guards all assumed someone else had gone in and waited silently.

With that challenge cleared, they all relaxed. Only Mamako seemed perturbed.

"We didn't even give them their Puff-Puffs! Is that okay?"

"It absolutely is. Like they said, being tricked is part of the Puff-Puff. That is the core nature of it. Everyone knows that. There's beauty in formula."

"I wish you'd let me be tricked..." Masato grumbled.

"I can feel hostility radiating from you, but look on the bright side. Over there! The entrance to adventure awaits!"

"Don't try to distract me! *Sigh...* Fine, whatever, I'll try to forget it happened."

He could still feel it on his face, so he slapped his cheeks and tried to focus.

They were in a small room. There was nothing in it but the stairs heading down.

"There are ancient ruins below us... Cool, cool, I can feel some nice savory tension building. We can finally have some fun! This is the adventure I've been waiting for! A proper dungeon!"

Masato ran off down the stairs...

...but a few steps down he paused and turned back.

"Oh, right. We don't need to pretend we're staff anymore. This room might be a good place to change. So why don't you all change before you follow me?"

"Change? Mommy was planning on going like this!"

"You're the one I most want to get changed! Take a hint!"

They were past security, and it was time to end the horror of having his mother dressed like a Bunny Girl. With that, Masato ran off down the stairs.

And thus, he beheld the casino depths.

CHUTES AND MOTHERS

3

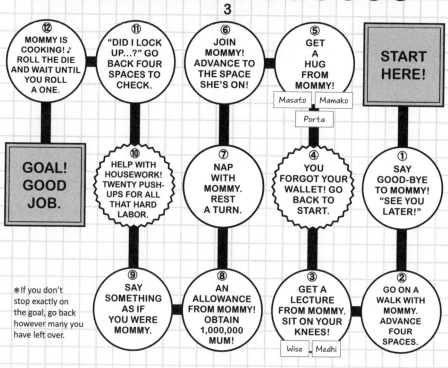

⑫ MOMMY IS COOKING! ♪ ROLL THE DIE AND WAIT UNTIL YOU ROLL A ONE.

⑪ "DID I LOCK UP...?" GO BACK FOUR SPACES TO CHECK.

⑥ JOIN MOMMY! ADVANCE TO THE SPACE SHE'S ON!

⑤ GET A HUG FROM MOMMY!

Masato | Mamako

Porta

START HERE!

GOAL! GOOD JOB.

⑩ HELP WITH HOUSEWORK! TWENTY PUSH-UPS FOR ALL THAT HARD LABOR.

⑦ NAP WITH MOMMY. REST A TURN.

④ YOU FORGOT YOUR WALLET! GO BACK TO START.

① SAY GOOD-BYE TO MOMMY! "SEE YOU LATER!"

✳ If you don't stop exactly on the goal, go back however many you have left over.

⑨ SAY SOMETHING AS IF YOU WERE MOMMY.

⑧ AN ALLOWANCE FROM MOMMY! OBTAIN 1,000,000 MUM!

③ GET A LECTURE FROM MOMMY. SIT ON YOUR KNEES!

Wise | Medhi

② GO ON A WALK WITH MOMMY. ADVANCE FOUR SPACES.

 Mommy gets a two! Oh no! I lose a turn.

 Um...um... I-I'm your mama! Let me spoil you rotten!

 My turn! I get... Aw... A two...

 I get a six! Six spaces forward takes me to nine... Huh? Hey!!

 ...Sigh...

 So Porta also loses a turn. Then I get... Ugh... A four...

Everyone, silence please. A word from Mama Wise.

 Medhiii! Knock it off with the meaningful sighs! Wait, you rolled a five?! You get a one-million-mum allowance?!

 Yes! Now Masato's on square nine, too! Hurry up and say something mama-like!

Chapter 4 Housework Is a Mother's Battleground. But If a Son Puts His Mind to It... Ack! Stop That!

The basement could not be less like the ultra-gaudy casino above.

The ancient ruins passage was shrouded in darkness, and they could barely see a step in front of them.

As much as he'd like to blame the darkness for his difficulty walking...

"...Mom, you're not making this easier."

"Oops, I'm so sorry. But Mommy just feels so happy when she's holding your arm like this. Hee-hee." *Sparkle!*

"With Mamako's A Mother's Light, we can see quite clearly."

"When Mama is happy or having fun, it activates automatically! Amazing!"

...only Masato was having trouble moving. But this was a necessary evil. He tried his best not to let her trip him up.

The party was back in their normal equipment, progressing down a corridor made of stones that were clearly ravaged by time. It twisted and turned like a labyrinth, but they were at no risk of getting lost.

After all, it never once branched.

"Oh! There's a fork up ahead! What now?"

"Don't worry. That's why we have Mamako...and Masato."

"Oh? I can help?"

"And me?" Masato asked, surprised.

"Haven't you noticed, Masato?" Shiraaase said softly. "It seems Mamako has acquired a new skill. I'm an admin, I can tell."

"What, really?"

"With this skill, we can easily get through this maze. But from what I've heard, for that skill's effect to activate properly, she needs to spoil you, so... Masato."

"Never. Seriously, not worth it."

"This is not time for quibbling. We're in a hurry! Come, Masato!"

"Argh... Fine! I'll do it! ...Mom!"

He took the arm she had locked with his and squeezed it tight.

"Oh my! You're even letting me spoil you here? Hee-hee."

Mamako's spoil gauge was charged up, and her unique skill, A Mother's Spoiling, received an effect boost!

As a result, the dungeon's difficulty level was dulled, and the three branches of the fork ahead twisted and merged into just a single path. Now they wouldn't get lost.

"What's the point in there even being a dungeon? ...This skill is straight-up broken... Please patch it..."

"I certainly see your point, but it works to our advantage."

"Thanks to Mama, we can move through this dungeon with ease! Nothing will stop us now!"

"Well, Ma-kun, let's all keep going! Yay!"

Mamako's skill certainly made things snappy.

But this was still a dungeon. And ancient ruins, too.

"...Oh, monsters!" Porta pointed ahead of them.

Spirits in ancient folk costumes stared at them with hollow eyes.

"Oh my goodness! Ghosts!"

"Yo, wait, there are monster spawns here?"

"It is an ancient ruin. Absolutely the type of dungeon where you would find undead monsters wandering for all eternity."

"Definitely the sort of thing you should warn us about ahead of time! *Tch!* Guess we have to fight!"

Masato took a firm grip on Firmamento and ran forward. Finally, his moment to shine! He wasn't a hero for nothing! He'd make it look easy!

But before he did, the ghosts started talking to Mamako.

"Oh, hey. Thanks for coming!"

"There's a pitfall just ahead, so make sure you don't fall in!"

"That happened to a skeleton just the other day! Walking on legs must be so rough."

"Why, thank you! We really appreciate the heads-up."

Their detection facilities spoiled, the ghosts didn't even realize they were enemies and floated away.

Masato quietly put his sword away. He wasn't crying. Not one tear!

"...Shiraaase, at this rate, I feel like we're never gonna fight enemies again."

"It certainly seems that way, but... How is that different from before? ...Oh?" Shiraaase suddenly stopped in her tracks. "Masato, did you hear that? I thought I heard a voice..."

"A voice...?"

Masato stopped, listening closely.

"......Hey.......... What?! ....Arghhhhh!......"

He couldn't make out much, but it sounded like a woman's voice.

"Doesn't seem like monsters... Wonder who it is...? Anyway, they're up ahead..."

As they moved forward, the voice got louder.

"......You can't even do that? ...How pathetic are you?!......"

"......I lost again! ...Why me?! ...This is your fault!......"

It was only women talking—or more accurately, screaming. They seemed to be quite beside themselves.

One section of the wall had a section cut out like a window. The voices were coming through it.

Masato ran up and peered through.

"...Um... What...the...?"

Far below them was what looked like an arena. They could see a circular ring made of old rock lit by the sinister light of magic stones.

Only women were sitting in the stands, each of them clutching scraps of paper.

And there were women in the ring, too. It was hard to make out what they were doing at this distance...but they were standing by a slab covered in bits of cloth, their hands moving quickly.

"Oh my, what is that...?"

"They're very excited, but what they're saying is really mean! ...Ms. Shiraaase! What are they doing?!" asked Porta.

"I'm afraid I'm not quite sure. I only thought they were hiding Alzare down here, but...given the foul language and competitive vibe, I believe they're betting on something. And getting worked up to a downright unnatural degree."

"In the ancient ruins under a casino, a whole lot of women gathered to gamble... What the heck? ...Hmm... All women, huh?"

An idea came to him, so Masato activated his mother-detection skill, A Child's Sense.

When he looked at the arena again, the women in the ring and in the stands were all giving off a carnation glow. Which meant...

"You've gotta be kidding me... They're moms. All of them."

"What?! They are?!"

"Ma-kun's fabulous skill means it must be true! Well done, Ma-kun! Mommy's so proud!"

"A skill that allows you to tell if a woman is a mother or not... Compared to Mamako's skill that spoils literally anything, that's, well... I suppose it's nice in its own way."

"Right, thanks for the input! You've made your point loud and clear, Shiraaase! I know that better than anyone. Please don't rub it in!"

But this made no sense.

Deep in an ancient ruin patrolled by undead monsters...a whole lot of mothers had gathered to gamble like crazy.

This wasn't right.

"We've got one of the Four Heavenly Kings of the Libere Rebellion, and she's got an item that can control NPCs and these mothers here... Clearly, the situation is worse than we thought."

"Then we'll have to do something about it!"

"That's our job!"

"This is, indeed, unexpected, but I'd like to request an emergency quest. Mamako, Porta, companions thereof, please accept it."

"You can't get me that easily! I'm onto you now, Shiraaase! You're doing that deliberately! *Sniff...* Let's go."

Heroes didn't cry. His eyes were glistening because his body's regular secretion of tears was simply functioning slightly higher than normal.

They ran off, searching for the stairs farther down.

Meanwhile, back at the casino:

"I'm goin' in! Bwaaaahhh! Pretty Bunny Kick!"

After a short sprint, Wise broke down the door with a dropkick utterly devoid of anything resembling cuteness and entered the manager's office.

Medhi came with her, utterly appalled.

"*Sigh*... I feel like you've lost the intelligence required to count as human, Wise..."

" I have not! I'm just really pissed off right now! I mean—!"

"You fought one of the Four Heavenly Kings and were brutally defeated. Such a shame!" *Snicker.*

"No, no, no, I won! I was cuter than Amante!"

"The crowd said otherwise. A loss is a loss... Well, it stands to reason. The kind of appeal you have only works with paid escorts. That whiff of criminality caused your downfall."

"Argh... Maybe I shouldn't have called those customers Daddy..."

"But what does it matter? The result is that we made enough money to pay back our debts."

"Oh! I'm kinda pissed about that, too! You didn't even ask! You just turned us into a show and let the money roll in! And... Huh?"

Wise suddenly realized there was one other person in the room with them.

It was the elderly assistant manager. Their sudden noisy intrusion neither surprised nor angered him; he simply stood there smiling.

He was such a calming presence that both girls instantly quieted down. They both bowed their heads to him.

"Um... H-hey there. Sorry to barge in like this."

"We apologize for the commotion. We've just repaid our debt at the prize exchange counter and were told to make an appearance here."

"Yes, I'm well aware. I'm afraid the manager is currently unavailable, so I'm serving in her stead. First, if I may just verify things..."

He reached out his hand to Wise and Medhi—that was all.

"Very good. Your debt is paid, and I've confirmed you've been set to your original jobs once more. Congratulations."

"Whew. Thanks... Uh, what did you just do?"

"Was that some sort of magic...?"

"I certainly do enjoy the odd spell or two, but this was nothing like that. I directly accessed your data and checked the contents. This is a game, after all, so operations like that take but a moment. The gesture is purely theatrical."

"Wh-whoa…"

"I suppose so, but…I feel like if you don't at least use an analysis spell, it really breaks the fourth wall…"

"Ha-ha-ha, I'll concede that point." His smile was so warm it was impossible to resent him. "Now, as you are both free once more, what are you planning to do next?"

"Good question…" said Wise. "I figured we'd start by finding Mamako and the others… They headed off toward the staff dorm but never came back."

"Yes… It's been an awfully long time… I wonder if something happened to them?"

"Would you mind if we discuss that further?"

"Huh? …D'you know something?"

"I certainly do. I am aware of everything that occurs within the territory assigned to me. That is my function, you see."

"Function? …Pardon me, but just who are—?"

"I'll save explanations about my nature for another time… At this moment, I've been granted a number of extra rights, so this is our chance. I shall explain about the basement, about the location of the item the admins are searching for, how your friends are helping to search for it…and about the sinister actions taken by Sorella. This is all my modest form of rebellion."

The assistant manager picked up the papers left abandoned on the desk and began to explain.

Masato's group continued deeper into the dungeon, running down corridor after corridor, looking for descending staircases.

"Careful! More monsters!"

"Cool, I'll—!"

"Mm? You're in a hurry? Go ahead!"

"Thanks for stepping aside! Ma-kun, come on!"

"Dammiiiiiit!"

The path never branched. The monsters all let them pass. Nothing blocked their progress. They just kept heading down staircase after staircase.

"We're getting pretty deep now. We must be nearly there..." said Shiraaase.

"Oh! There's a gate ahead of us!" cried Porta.

"It seems we're almost at our destination. The arena of mothers may be beyond that gate."

"Cool! Then I'll take the lead! Leave this to me!"

Masato sped up, running through the arched gate before any minions were spoiled.

Beyond it, he found the circular arena they'd seen from above. He'd come through a passage leading to the stage.

Weird.

"H-huh? ...There's nobody here...?"

There were a number of tables lined up, with sewing kits and cloth laid out on them. That's what it had looked like from a distance, but...

...the people were gone. The stands were equally deserted. Not one mother remained.

Masato's group stepped up onto the stage for a better view...but they were definitely alone.

"Yo, what's going on here?"

"There's no one around... I wonder if they all went somewhere?" wondered Mamako.

"M-maybe what we saw were some mommy ghosts! Yiiiikes...!"

"All the monsters we've seen *have* been undead, after all. I think it is certainly possible that those mothers were the ghosts of ancient people who lived in these ruins, but...would ghosts really be sewing things?"

Shiraaase picked up a badly sewn appliqué with a cute bunny on it, thinking.

Then:

"Ohhh, you're already heeere. I had a feeling this would haaappen. And here I was hoping you would just go awaaay. Waaah, waahhh."

The group turned toward the voice. It was coming from the box seats above the stands.

Sorella was seated there, languidly watching them.

"Arghhh! Aaargh, arghhh! Why did you have to coooome?! This suuuucks!"

"Heroes always arrive when villains least want them to. And I am a hero. Ha-ha!"

"A spoiled boy who begged his mother for chips is trying to act all coooool. Some heroooo."

"Says the member of the Four Heavenly Kings who looked down on my mom and lost a fortune."

Spitting venom, both were getting equally worked up. It was a draw.

Sorella pretended she hadn't heard that last bit and spoke languidly, trying to appear confident.

"Then I suppose I should say hellooo... Hiiii! Thank you, thank youuu. Mamakoooo! Masatooo! Portaaa! Shiraaase from admiiiin! Welcome, all of youuu. Well, not actually welcome, buuuut...I've arranged something of a welcome paaarty!"

Sorella snapped her fingers.

Two skeletons appeared beside her, dressed like knights.

They were holding up a banner that read simply: HASINO.

At the same time, women with shopping baskets began filing into the stands, which were soon completely full. "Those are..." Masato quickly checked with A Child's Sense. Everyone had that carnation glow. These women were all mothers.

Sorella looked over the assembled mothers, all grimacing fiercely, and said, "Okaaay, we're open for buuuusiness. Everyone claaap!"

The mothers burst into applause. It was deafening. Overwhelming.

Even Masato found himself clapping, joining in. Hang on.

"Wait, you spelled *casino* wrong. It's supposed to start with a C."

"I spelled it riiight! This is place iiiiis... Well, you don't need to know, Masatooo. This is a secret place for moms to plaaay. Soooo..."

Sorella glared fiercely down at Masato and Porta.

As she did, their shadows rose up off the ground and grabbed hold of them.

"What?!" "Whoa!" They were dragged down off the stage and toward the exit.

"Wh-what the...? Hey! Lemme go!"

"Hngg! I can't move!"

"I put ghosts in your shadooows. I'm actually a Necromancer, you seeee. I can do these thiiings. Alsooo…my skill is absolutely actiiiive, so your skills are dropping and you can't fiiight. Pffft."

"You've certainly got us there…" said Shiraaase.

"Ma-kun?! Porta?! I'll save you!"

"I won't let youuu!"

Sorella snapped her fingers again. Instantly, a tall fence sprang up around the stage, trapping Mamako and Shiraaase inside.

"The two mothers will find participation is maaandatoryyy."

"You're quite a piece of work."

"Sorella, please! Won't you be kind enough to let us through? Please!"

"No need to act all desperaaate. I'm not taking your children awaaay. I'll just hold on to them a whiiile."

"H-hey! This isn't a hostage thing, is it? Think about how bad that makes me look!"

"Grrr! I don't like people who are mean to Mama!"

"Ohhh, shut uuuup! I've got to explain things to the mothers nooow. Go awaaay!"

"Hey, wait! Seriously, don't! In this instance, I don't mind risking my life! I'm the hero here. I can't be the one getting rescued, especially by my own mother! That's completely unacceptable! Ahhhh… Ahhhhh…!"

But his fate was already decided. He was a hostage.

Masato and Porta were dragged away.

Mamako desperately stretched her arms through the fence but could not reach them.

She swayed, about to crumple to her knees, but Shiraaase caught her in time.

"Mamako, hang in there. If you want to get them back, you have to keep your wits about you."

"R-right! I can do this!"

"Yes, you can. I won't be very useful here. I lack the ability or the motivation. So we're relying on you here."

Shiraaase quietly abdicated all participation.

The two mothers turned and glared at Sorella.

"...So time for that explanation?" asked Shiraaase.

"Yes, yeees. About thaaaat. A demonstration is always better than a dreary explanaaaation... Will the previous champion step onto the staaage?"

A mother stood up from the crowd and came down the aisle.

One section of the fence briefly dropped, and the mother stepped into the ring. She was wearing ordinary clothes and an apron and held a pile of men's shirts tightly in both hands.

She looked for all the world like she was in the middle of doing laundry—were it not for the grim aura pulsing around her.

"And this is...?"

"Mamako, be careful. This is the arena champion. It is possible those shirts are her weapons, and she'll attack with a highly unorthodox fighting style."

Hackles raised, Shiraaase took a step back, hiding behind Mamako.

The mother faced her, eyes fierce.

"I have nothing against you! But this is a competition!" she shouted.

"A competition? This is so sudden...!"

"Doesn't matter! Prepare yourself!"

The next moment, the mother's arms swung wide...

...and softly placed one of the shirts in Mamako's hands.

"The one who folds this fastest and best wins. Ready! Start!"

"Huh? Oh, okay... What?"

Mamako seemed rather baffled by this.

But the competition had already begun! Both mothers quickly dropped to their knees, spread out the shirts across their laps, and began folding!

The champion mother was not, honestly, particularly good. She folded the hem and then said, "Oh, I should start with the sleeves!" and started over, folding the sleeves, but they were all rumpled so she started over once again...

Meanwhile, Mamako, who had plenty of practice folding Masato's shirts, finished hers up too fast for the eye to follow.

"Will this do?"

"Allow me to check. Hmm... Left and right are even, size is right... Flawless!"

"R-really?! That was way too fast! And so skillfull!"

Mamako had folded the shirt so neatly that it looked just like something on display at a clothing store. The other mother conceded defeat, hung her head, and went back to the stands.

Mamako defeated the arena champion, becoming the new champion! But she seemed utterly confused by the whole thing.

"Um... Shiraaase, what just happened?"

"I have no idea. Perhaps the person in charge would care to explain?"

They both turned toward the box seat.

Sorella seemed displeased by Mamako's victory, but she recovered.

"Okaaay... Then I'll explaaain," she said. "It's basically like what you just diiid. Mothers face off on that staaage, the crowd bets on who will wiiin, then the winner gets a priiize. That's basically iiit."

"So it's a mom-off?"

"Yeeesss. You battle in housewooork. This is a Hasino—a housework casinoooo."

"So... A house casino... A house-ino... A hasino. I admire your naming sense, at least," said Shiraaase.

"Thaaanks... Honestly, I wanted to make them fight with swooords. But they all just said, 'But we caaan't.' So I had them decide how they wanted to fiiight. And it ended up like thiiis."

Sorella's sleepy eyes narrowed as a malicious smile played over her lips.

"They aren't strong enough to fight with swords, so they're competing with housewooork. Isn't that so duuumb? What a waste of tiiime. They're all so stuuupid. But these mothers mean busineeess. They're blinded by the prizes and trying so haaard. Mothers getting all worked up over something like that is so funnyyy. Mwa-ha-haaa."

"Wait. That's hardly a laughing matter."

"Mocking the efforts of mothers... As a mother myself, I find that most unpleasant."

"I feel just great about iiit. I mean, I'm one of the Four Heavenly Kings of the Libere Rebelliiion, Scorn-Mom Sorella, she who scorns all mooothers. Why wouldn't I heap indignities upon theeem? It really makes me feel aliiive. Mwa-ha-haaa."

That was definitely a laugh of pure glee.

Mamako's index finger shot out, her other hand at her hip, ready to scold. "Wait," Shiraaase said. "Mamako, calm down. This is not the moment to act."

"But if she isn't given a proper scolding..."

"Remember, she has Masato and Porta captive. We need to bide our time and wait for an opportunity."

"O-oh, right..."

Mamako lowered her finger.

Sorella had tensed up, but she sighed with relief and looked confident again.

"Then let's get staaarted. These are one-on-one maaatches. Either Mamako or Shiraaase will fight the chaaallenger. Recruiting challengers from the crooowd. Anyone who wants a prize, join iiin. And as for the priiize..."

There was a drumroll from somewhere, and the knight skeletons lowered a banner.

DESIGNER BAG AND WALLET

The moment this was revealed—"I'm in!" "Me too!" "No, me!"—yes, yes, yes, yes! The crowd exploded. Such desire!

Sorella doubled over laughing.

"Bwa-ha-ha-ha-haaa! Th-they're so exciiited! Please, it's too muuuch! I can't stop laughing at the sheer greeed! Haaah! I'm dying heeere! ...*Gasp, gaaasp...* R-right, you in the stands, get down to the staaage!"

Sorella seemed to have picked the challenger at random. The chosen mother grabbed her shopping basket, hastily rose to her feet, and came hustling out of the stand, all eyes on her.

She stood before Mamako and Shiraaase.

"Well, Motheeer, which would you fight?"

"I'd like to fight Mamako! I want to beat her and become the new champion! All the prizes will be mine!"

"Wait! I don't want to fight anyone—!"

"Ohhhh? You don't care what happens to Masato and Portaaa?"

"Mamako, this is no time for principles. Think of the children!"

"If you put it that way, I suppose I have no choice..."

"And no letting her off easyyy. These fights aren't funny if you aren't trying your beeest... Well, Motherrrr? What will you fight her iiiin?"

"Cabbage julienning!"

The mother pulled two half cabbages and a julienne slicer out of her basket, clearly intending to use the specialized tool to ensure her victory.

"Bwa-ha-haaa! Another extremely drab, domestic conteeest! ...Now, everyooooone. Place your beeeets! If you win, you get double your bet baaack! Come ooon!"

A large number of ghosts began moving swiftly through the crowds, exchanging ballot tickets for whatever the crowd was betting.

The mothers were betting all sorts of things. "My clothes!" "These seasonings!" "Twelve rolls of toilet paper!" All sorts of everyday items they must have brought from home in their baskets. This seemed to amuse Sorella to no end.

Many, many bets were placed, and time was called.

"Okay, okaaay, who will our victor beee? Let's begiiin. Will Mamako and the challenger please take your placeeeees? ... Readyyyy... *Bang!*"

With that, the battle began. Mamako and the mother each ran to the nearest counter.

The challenger set the cabbage on the slicer—*chop, chop, chop*—julienning the vegetable with ease. Using a tool definitely made it fast.

But next to her...

"*Hyah!*"

...Mamako's kitchen knife sliced rapid-fire and her half cabbage was all chopped in the blink of an eye.

Mamako won! But she seemed very apologetic.

"Um, I'm sorry about that. I just thought it would be rude to hold back..."

"Su-sure, that's fine, but...my slicer is so fast...and I accidentally bought three of them so I was so hoping it would prove itself here... Sigh..."

Dejected, the mother slumped back to the stands.

Sorella looked disappointed.

"Ughhh... Mamako wooon. How duuuull. We'll give out the prizes laaater. Next baaattle! ...Okay... You, the mother over theeere. You're neeext."

The mother selected at random came running toward the stage with two brooms in her hands.

"Mamako! Let's battle over cleaning this stage!"

"I suppose I must... Very well!"

Another round of household goods was exchanged for tickets. "I'm betting on Mamako!" "I'm backing the challenger!" "Me too!" It seemed the odds were in favor of the challenger this time.

The battle began.

"I'll clean the right half of the stage, and you take the left! Ready, start!"

"Oh—!"

The challenging mother was already cleaning—bits of thread and scraps of cloth, remains of different kinds of food, all the refuse left upon the stage was swept quickly away—paying no heed to how the wind pressure scattered the heap of garbage behind her.

"Ha-ha-ha! Sweeping in squares is a core technique! It's just common sense!"

The mother was using straight lines and right angles, diligently sweeping one square at time...

...but half the stage of a circular arena was a semicircle.

"O-oh... Huh? This isn't working!"

"Heh... That should do nicely."

As the challenger reeled, Mamako finished! Not a speck of dust remaining on her side. "And these metal scraps are nonburnable." She'd even sorted the types of trash!

Mamako wins!

"Um, try not to take it too hard, okay? We all fail sometimes!"

"You're so nice... But a loss is a loss... I thought I had it, too..."

The defeated mother retreated.

"Hey! What was that? I bet on you!"

"Who forgets the shape of the space they're sweeping?! Your sweeping skill is sorely lacking!"

"I should've gone in your place! Give me back what I bet!"

The other moms began mercilessly booing the defeated mother. "Um, please, just a minute…" Mamako tried to step in, but…

…her voice was drowned out by Sorella's cackle.

"Ah-ha-ha-haaa! Mothers are so funnyyy! Hilaaaarious!"

"She did her best! Laughing at her isn't—"

"No, noooo! That's not the poooint… What's funny isn't that she looost, it's the way the other mothers forget that they're in the same boat and yell at heeer! Who do they think they aaare?! Pfffftt!"

The crowd of moms twitched simultaneously and shut their mouths.

Sorella laughed until she was out of breath, her eyes drunk on mirth. She looked around the crowd.

"Let me tell youuuu. None of the mothers heeere…are doing any housewooork. They're spending all day gaaambling. But they think they have the right to sneer at otheeers! Even though they're all lousy moooooms. It's too funnyyy!"

"They've been here this whole time…?"

"Are you using some illicit means? That's the only possibility I can only imagine…" said Shiraaase.

"No, no, nooo! I haven't done a thiiing! I simply extended a kind offer to the town mothers, ones who usually never set foot inside a casinooo. Their minds… Hmm… I didn't mess with them muuuch? I mean…seeing how useless ordinary mothers are is so much more fuuun. Go ooon. Keep making me laaaugh. Next mother to the staaaage!"

Sorella picked a new contestant, who took the stage.

But before the next fight, Shiraaase made a suggestion.

"Mamako, would you mind if I handled the next one? It seems fighting other mothers is a terrible burden upon you."

"Oh, that would be so nice of you…"

"And if we're fighting mothers who never do housework, even I stand a good chance. If I can win, I'm happy to fight."

"Wow, how brazen of you!"

"So I would like to infooorm you that I, Shiraaase, will fight the next battle! Any objections, manager?"

"Do whateeever... Challenging Motheeer! What is our competitiooon?"

"I'd like a button-sewing battle!"

Ballots were quickly distributed. The battle began.

"Readyyy... Start!"

At Sorella's signal, Shiraaase and the mother ran to their counters, snatching up the cloth and sewing kits.

The challenger mother didn't seem to be very handy with housework and was struggling to thread her needle...

"Done. I win," Shiraaase said.

She proudly held up a cloth, with a button held in place...by a safety pin.

This wasn't a matter of being good or bad at sewing.

Silence settled over the arena, a prelude to a fierce round of booing...

But Mamako started clapping.

"Amazing, Ms. Shiraaase! Such an avant-garde way of fastening!"

"I am honored by your praise. Once before, I fastened my daughter's clothing this way, and she was delighted. 'Mommy, that's so punk rock!' she said. I may not be that skilled at housework, but I still feel like I make a fine mother, and this incident merely confirmed as much."

"Hee-hee. That's lovely. Housework isn't about being good or bad, it's about pleasing those you live with. That's what matters most. That's what brings us joy."

Shiraaase nodded emphatically.

The mothers in the crowd lowered the fists they'd been about to raise. Mamako and Shiraaase had clearly given them a lot to think about...

But Sorella's disgruntled voice cut through the calm.

"Right, riiight! We don't need any talk like thaaat! Crappy mothers will always be crappyyyy! Disgrace yourselves for my pleasuuure! Keep on suuucking! Neeext..."

She got ready to pick the next challenger.

However...

"U-um, Ms. Sorella! Can I ask something?"

...a mother in the stands had raised her hand. She was trembling.

"Mm? Who are youuu? If you want somethiiiing, you'll have to introduce yourself fiiirst. I can't be bothered remembering any of youuu."

"R-right! I'm the mother from the general store on the outskirts of the commercial district! Um... After that last battle, I've run out of things to bet..."

"You haaave? I see, I seee... Wait... The general stooore? Oh, right, okaaay! I was waiting for thiiis! You seee, there's actually a bonus challenge you can joiiin. We'll get it ready for you right awaaay. Mwa-ha-haaa."

Sorella seemed thoroughly pleased with herself. Like nothing could be better.

"...Ms. Shiraaase..."

"Yes... This doesn't sound good..."

But however sinister this might be, trapped inside the fence without their weapons, there was nothing either could do to stop it.

Bound by their own shadows, Masato and Porta were dragged down the passageway.

"Dammit! Lemme go! Please, I'm begging you!"

"Hnggg! ...Aw... I can't move..."

Even trying to resist felt futile. They were dragged helplessly onward and onward...

...and then a moment later they were pulled into a room.

"H-huh? We stopped moving. What is this room? ...Hey! Are we locked in here?!"

"Eep! Masato, look around us! There are so many children!"

"Huh? Children?"

He was still bound by his shadow, so all he could move was his head.

But when he looked around, he saw the room filled was with stuffed animals of all shapes and sizes and maybe ten children, all younger than Porta.

One little boy came toddling over to them. He stared up at Masato with big round eyes.

"Hey, mister, who are you?" he asked.

"I'm, uh… Well, it's kinda hard to call myself a hero when I'm trapped like this…"

"Hmm, I don't get it… What are you doing?"

"What am I…? H-hey, I could ask you the same question. Why are you all here?"

"Um, I was playing outside, and a man in black came, and he said Mommy was waiting for me. I dunno why, but he brought me here. It's the same for all of us."

"You don't know why? …Ohhh, maybe they're controlling you… But gathering kids here and telling them their mothers are waiting for them…"

The man in black must be a casino guard. Or something like that, anyway.

It seemed likely that these kids belonged to the mothers in the arena.

"If they went to all the trouble of taking them here, they must be planning on doing something with them… And nothing good, either…"

So he had to stop it. Obviously.

But if he was going to do that, the first thing he had to do was free himself from this shadow. This was his top priority…

But then he heard voices on the other side of the door:

"…This is the room where the kids are locked up, right? C'mon! I'm gonna kick it in!…"

"…Wait! There might be a child near the door!…"

"…Oh, true… Don't wanna hurt or scare them… Okay…"

The door slooowly opened, and a pair of bunny ears entered first, wobbling.

Smiling like the hosts of a children's TV program, Wise and Medhi came hopping in.

"Hello, everybunny! We're two cute little wabbits and… Uh… Huh?"

"No need to be scaredy-bunnies! Just listen to us and… Um…"

They both froze, recognizing their friends.

Masato averted his eyes.

"Don't mind me," he said. "I'll pretend I wasn't looking. As you were."

"We can't now! This is super-awkward! And why are you even—? Oh, Porta, you're here, too!"

"Yes! I am! Should I also pretend I didn't see that?"

"I-if you could be so kind..." said Medhi. "But what's going on here? You seem to be tied up with some sort of shadow... Oh no, it's an undead type of monster... Then..."

Medhi pointed at the shadows binding them and chanted a spell.

"...*Spara la magia per mirare... Purificare!*"

A purifying light gathered on Medhi's palm, illuminating all the dead things skulking about.

The sinister shadows vanished instantly, freeing Masato and Porta.

"Whoa! Thanks!"

"Medhi, thank you! You saved us!"

"You're welcome. I'm glad I could help."

"No, seriously, you saved our... Wait, Medhi, I thought you couldn't use magic?"

"Well, I might still look like a Bunny Girl, but we've paid off our debt and had our jobs restored. So I can use magic again... And I don't actually need my staff!"

"The free-cast on random spells is handy, but come to think of it, otherwise I've only ever seen you use the staff to hit things."

"None of that matters! I demand an explanation! Masato, what the heck?!" shouted Wise.

"Oh yeah, uh... Calm your cotton tail, bunny."

"I *will* kill you."

Now that Wise could use magic again, she got ready to chain cast— "No magic!" "Physical attacks okay, then?!" Clearly having Masato witness the whole bunny talk thing had left her a little red-faced, a problem she solved by hitting him in the head with her magic tome.

Medhi healed him after, and they traded stories.

They left the crowd of confused children to Porta. Masato filled Wise and Medhi in on their side of things, and the girls explained what had happened to them.

Once they were all caught up...

"The assistant manager sure seems to know a lot... But it sounds like we've got three tasks ahead of us."

"Let the children go, help Mamako and Shiraaase in the arena, and recover this Alzare thing."

"Handling them one at a time might be safer, but it sounds like they're all connected, so I'd prefer to tackle them all at once," added Medhi.

"Yep... Hmm..."

This wasn't something easily done. Masato knew that.

But looking at Wise and Medhi like this, he remembered how the three of them had sat on the ground, watching Mamako mow down all the monsters.

I'd like to handle this ourselves...for the sake of our pride.

Perhaps they knew what he was thinking. They both looked at him expectantly.

In which case...

"We gotta kick things up a notch."

"That's what I'm talkin' about!"

"Naturally."

Masato held out a fist, and Wise and Medhi both bumped it.

A war on three fronts awaited.

"There's no time to sit and chat," said Masato. "Let's do the rundown."

"We just gotta get the kids to the casino safely. The assistant manager will handle them from there. If we get them that far without a hitch, we're in the clear."

"We've also pinpointed the location of the Alzare. The assistant manager gave us a map, so I think it's the shortest route."

"As for helping Mom and Shiraaase... Well, we got kicked out for being kids... There must be some way of getting closer to the stage... Hmm?"

As he was racking his brains for an idea, the door opened again.

In came a skeleton dressed in a rabbit costume, its body fluffy and face bony. "A monster!" "Eeeek!" The children all started screaming. No surprise there.

Masato's group jumped to their defense.

"Wha—?! That's creepy! We'd better fight... Wait, it's not attacking?"

The skeleton was just standing peacefully in the doorway.

It looked around at all the children, checking several times, then said, "...Child from the general store, on the commercial district's outskirts... Come with me to the arena..."

Apparently it had come for one specific child.

But it didn't seem to know who that child was. It looked around, repeating the same line... Maybe it was wearing this costume so as to not frighten them? It seemed to have backfired...

"...Um, mister..."

"Y-yeah?"

The boy who'd spoken to them before tugged on Masato's leg. He seemed to be hiding behind Masato so the skeleton wouldn't find him.

"Oh, are you the general store kid?" Masato whispered.

The boy nodded, looking ready to cry.

This gave Masato an idea.

"...Hey, Wise. You can use transformation magic, right?"

"Uh, yeah, technically..."

"Then let's use that. Lend me your ear."

He meant to whisper his idea...but Wise just took her bunny ears off and handed them to him. "Here." "Yeah, that's what I meant! If I equip those... Wait, no! Not those!" "Yeah, I know." This really wasn't the time for dumb jokes.

This was their chance to act.

Back in the arena, some time had passed since Sorella's ominous proclamation.

Trapped on the stage, Mamako and Shiraaase remained concerned, watching their surroundings carefully.

"Whatever she's planning...is certainly taking a great deal of time..." said Mamako.

"If nothing happens, that's certainly not a bad thing," replied Shiraaase. "...Oh? Is that...?"

Someone had emerged from the passage: the general store mother and a little boy. They were led toward the stage by a skeleton in a rabbit costume.

From the box seats, Sorella crowed, "We're finally readyyy! You sure kept us waitiiing! Now let's begin the bonus rooound! ...General Store Mooom..."

"For this fight, you'll be betting your motherhooood!"

Mamako, Shiraaase, the mother in question, and everyone in the audience gasped.

Only Sorella was left smiling with delight.

"You'll be facing Mamakooo. And if you win the maaatch...I'll return everything you've bet so faaar. Yaaay, what a bonuuus! But if you loooose, you'll no longer be a motheeer... Well, General Store Mooom? What do you saaay?"

"U-um, by 'motherhood,' you mean...?"

"Exactly what it sounds liiiike! ...The casino upstairs has a special system that lets us temporarily change people's joooobs. If we use that with the Alzaaaare, we can make it so you aren't a motherrr. But we do need your conseeent."

At this, Mamako shouted, "Stop this at once! This is wrong! A mother is always a mother!"

"Now, noooow. Calm down, Mamakooo. I'm not hurting anybooody. The settings will make it so she was never a mooother, so neither she nor her kid will know they were ever relaaated. It will be a totally natural breakuuup. No teaaars. After all, this is just a gaaame."

"That's not the problem here! That's not it at all!"

"There is no proooblem. Not to meee. If a mother gambles away her identity as a mother then that's just funnyyy... And my rebelliiion? We'd love nothing more if mothers ceased to exist at aaaall... So let's begiiin!"

"No! You can't do this!"

"Audience, place your beeets. Will the general store mother take the challenge or noooot? What do you thiiink?"

Ignoring Mamako's pleas, ballots were distributed through the crowd.

Though upset, the mothers were still betting. "...She'll do it." "I...I agree." It seemed like many of them thought the general store mother would put her motherhood on the line.

Sorella appeared delighted by this.

"Yaaay! Everyone thinks you're gonna do iiit! They're all awful mothers, toooo! ...They know how you feeeel! ...Well, Mamakooo? What do you saaay?"

"What do you mean...?"

"Mamakooo, you might believe this NPC mother is a real motherrr but look at her noooow. Isn't it just unbearaaaable? Mothers are all—"

"I believe in her. I believe in the strength of a mother's feelings."

Mamako was resolute.

She turned and looked at the general store mother.

"Don't make this mistake. Don't rush into anything."

"Well... Look, I know this is wrong. But...but part of me thinks that even if I lose, that won't be so bad..."

"How can you—?"

"I mean, I *am* an awful mother... I can't quit gambling... And I was never good at cooking, cleaning, or laundry... I'm sure my boy would rather have someone else for a mother. He's better off without—"

"That's not true! Children always want their mothers! You have a mother yourself—you should know how your child feels!"

"Well... Yes, I suppose so... Even a mother like me has feelings..."

The general store mother mulled over what Mamako had said, looking somewhat mollified.

"No matter what an awful mother says, it won't change a thiiing. Don't disrupt her decisiooon."

Sorella jumped in, glaring at the skeleton in the rabbit suit. It shuffled into place between the general store mother and Mamako, blocking their conversation.

"Let's get this moviiing... General store motherrr! Say good-bye to your son, just in caaase. The moment you lose he'll be a strangerrr. Go on and look absolutely pathetic for my pleasuuure. Go aheeead... If you don't hurry, the skeleton might get angryyy."

"O-oh no...!" Frightened, the mother turned to her stunned-looking son. "U-um, so... Mama is... Mama's going to...!"

Twitching every time the skeleton moved, she tried to say something. But as she did...

"Mm."

...his face almost expressionless, the boy grabbed his mother's sleeve.

That was all it took.

That single action was enough to send a powerful shock through his mother.

"I...I can't do it! I can't stop being your mom! I may be an awful mother, but...but even so, if I can, I want to keep being your mom!"

She hugged the boy close, as if she'd never let him go again.

Many of the eyes watching her filled with tears.

The mothers in the stands didn't care that their expectations had been subverted; they just stared at the mother and her child. "If only we could be like that..." "Maybe there's still a chance for me..." Moved by the heartwarming sight, they began remembering forgotten emotions of their own.

Mamako was greatly relieved to see it. She nodded at Shiraaase.

Sorella's irritation reached its peak, and she opened her mouth to hurl further abuse...

...but before she could:

"I'm so relieved! I knew all mothers were mothers right down to their cores!" the boy said.

He spoke clearly, quite unlike his apparent age.

"Huh? ...That's not my boy's voice... Wh-who are you...?"

"I'm sorry! I'm actually not the general store child! I'm...!"

The transformation spell wore off.

A puff of smoke surrounded the child...and a female Traveling Merchant appeared, sporting her trademark shoulder bag.

The general store mother looked horrified, but there were those among the crowd who knew this girl.

"Oh my! That's Porta!" hollered Mamako.

"Porta, is that you?" Shiraaase called out.

"Yes! It's me! Wise cast a transformation spell on me!"

"Wise is here, too? And Medhi?" Mamako asked.

"Yes! They paid off their debts! And came to save me and Masato! All the children are safe! They're doing great!"

"It seems Masato and the other children are no longer hostages... Then..."

"You don't need to worry about anything! Nothing at all!" Porta started running. The skeleton tried to grab her, but she easily slipped past it. **"I'm gonna get you!"** "No, you won't!"

She dashed up to the stage and pulled two swords out of her bag, passing them through the gaps in the fence.

"Mama! Take it away!"

"Got it! Leave this to me!"

In her right hand, the Holy Sword of Mother Earth, Terra di Madre. In her left, the Holy Sword of Mother Ocean, Altura.

Taking a firm grip on each sword, Mamako swung them both.

Stone blades shot out of the earth, severing the fence. The hail of water bullets that followed utterly obliterated the rabbit-suited skeleton.

It was time to fight back.

"Sorella, are you ready? ...I've got a lecture with your name on it."

Mamako glared fiercely up at the stands.

Sorella gnashed her teeth in frustration, glaring back, but then she grinned.

"Ha-haaa... I don't need a lecture from any motherrr. I've got other ways of controlling youuu. Using this is against my philosophyyy... But I'm going to anywaaay."

Sorella waved a hand. In the air above her head appeared a magic tome the size of a tatami mat.

She opened the massive floating book, and a dull light shone from within, illuminating the stage, the stands, everything in sight...and a moment later, tiny little objects started welling up from everywhere.

Stone gambling chips. They flew around like swarms of insects, flitting past Mamako's face, buzzing in Shiraaase's ears.

"Oh dear! Nooo! This is bad!"

"Like flies or gnats... Definitely enough to make you want to kill."

"Mwa-ha haaa... You're helpless nooow! Serves you riiight!"

Batting them away with their hands did no good. They were exactly like the sort of bugs that invade the kitchen in summer. The most obnoxious creatures in the world.

The mothers in the stands were in a state. "Arghhh!" "Go away!" Flailing arms about, clapping hands to try to take them down, their battle raged. But the chips easily avoided their hands, fueling their frustration...

...and then:

"Aaah-ha-haaa! You're so desperaaate! But you can't get rid of themmm! Useless mothers can't do anythiiing! So funnyyy! Pfft!"

Peals of laughter echoed.

This really seemed to piss the moms off. Frustration peaking, their fists tightened. Insult upon insult was starting to provoke them into resistance.

In that moment:

"Everyone, listen to me!" Mamako's voice rang out. "What is a mother? Is a mother determined by her skills at cooking, cleaning, and laundry? If one slips up and starts gambling, is one no longer a mother? ...I say nay! Those things do not define a mother!"

To emphasize her words, Mamako swung both swords.

Terra di Madre's attack sent countless rock spikes out of the ground, piercing the swarming stone chips.

Altura's attack sent a volley of waterdrops that swept away everything nearby.

Her voice carried an important message:

"A mother's feelings are everything! Her feelings for her family are what make her a mother! Those feelings give us our strength! Remember how it feels! ...Remember the joy of eating with your family and how we respond when we see something flying across the dinner table! If something is buzzing around and scaring our children, what do we mothers do?"

When they heard these words, the mothers in the stands all sprang into action.

Each of them reached into their shopping baskets, took out flyers for grocery stores and drug stores, and rolled them into cylinders... Now they were armed.

"As a mother myself, I am honor bound to join this fight." Shiraaase picked up a nearby knitting needle from the stage and stood on guard.

Porta joined them. She produced a piece of wood and a board from her bag.

"Will it be good? It'll be good! A good item...done!"

Item Creation made...a flyswatter.

She ran over to the general store mother and placed the flyswatter in her hand.

"This is your time to fight as a mother! Here!"

"That's right! I may not be a great mother, but I still am one! I'll do whatever I can! I'll fight with everything I've got!"

The general store mother grabbed the flyswatter and took a firm grip on the handle.

They were mothers, and they would fight. Looking around her fierce army of mothers, Mamako raised her Holy Swords high.

"O Mothers Earth and Ocean... If you acknowledge your motherhood, then you understand how I feel... Should you grant us some sort of blessing, then I believe these mothers...all of them...could take a new step forward... For all us mothers who have sworn to fight, lend us your strength!"

In response, the two swords radiate warm lights.

These lights flew off like comets and entered the weapons in the mothers' hands. Rolled-up flyers, knitting needles, flyswatters—each one shone so bright it was blinding...

The rolled-up flyers became A Mother's Rolled-Up Flyer! The knitting needles became A Mother's Knitting Needles! The flyswatter became A Mother's Flyswatter!

Their appearance didn't change at all. But they were much stronger!

"Come, everyone! Let us show her we mothers mean business!"

The mothers let out a roar and rattled their weapons.

But their enemy smiled imperiously.

"All you moms are so worked uuuup. This is pointleeeess... But fiiine, I'll indulge youuu."

This scorn proved the final spark that set their hearts ablaze...

"Ah! Ms. Shiraaase, look out!"

"Oh?"

Except for one, who bumped her head on a stone chip and instantly became a coffin.

CHUTES AND MOTHERS

4

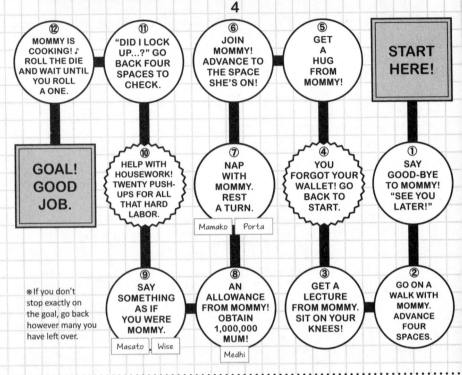

⑫ MOMMY IS COOKING! ♪ ROLL THE DIE AND WAIT UNTIL YOU ROLL A ONE.

⑪ "DID I LOCK UP...?" GO BACK FOUR SPACES TO CHECK.

⑥ JOIN MOMMY! ADVANCE TO THE SPACE SHE'S ON!

⑤ GET A HUG FROM MOMMY!

START HERE!

GOAL! GOOD JOB.

⑩ HELP WITH HOUSEWORK! TWENTY PUSH-UPS FOR ALL THAT HARD LABOR.

⑦ NAP WITH MOMMY. REST A TURN.

Mamako | Porta

④ YOU FORGOT YOUR WALLET! GO BACK TO START.

① SAY GOOD-BYE TO MOMMY! "SEE YOU LATER!"

※ If you don't stop exactly on the goal, go back however many you have left over.

⑨ SAY SOMETHING AS IF YOU WERE MOMMY.

Masato | Wise

⑧ AN ALLOWANCE FROM MOMMY! OBTAIN 1,000,000 MUM!

Medhi

③ GET A LECTURE FROM MOMMY. SIT ON YOUR KNEES!

② GO ON A WALK WITH MOMMY. ADVANCE FOUR SPACES.

 Mamako loses a turn, so it's me again! Okay! One! ...Oh, push-ups... Well, whatever.

 I can't believe you're resorting to working out to increase your bust size...

 I'm not! I mean, that'd be nice and all, but still!

 I got a three. Three forward... four back...lose a turn.

 I also lost a turn, so Masato's up next!

 Great! I got...a three! Three forward... Only one more space left, but I've gotta wait for the food to be ready!

 What should I make tonight? ... Oh, it's my turn. Goodness, I got a five! Same space as you, Ma-kun!

Chapter 5 Just Like with Gambling, the Greater the Appeal, the Greater the Risk. I Realized As Much from Watching Someone Close to Me.

Back to the child rescue team.

"C'mon, kids! Follow us! We'll keep you safe!"

"Wise may be a very pitiful person, but don't worry. I'm a lot nicer and much more competent, so I'll be the one keeping you safe."

"Medhi! Will you just cooperate for once?! Seal that dark heart away!"

Wise and Medhi were attempting to escape the ruins with a dozen children in tow.

But these children were quite small, and speed wasn't their strong suit. The two girls were forced to stifle the urge to rush them and instead kept pace with the children.

Then a group of monsters appeared in the passage ahead. What now?

"Wise, are you ready?"

"Okay! Leave it to me!"

Wise summoned her magic tome and leaped forward.

"I can actually use magic now, so trash mobs like these are easily..."

"*Wise's magic was sealed,*" Medhi whispered.

"What...the...? Ughhh, I'm so done..."

"Ah, Wise, Wise, I was kidding, okay? Don't take it seriously."

"Medhiiiiii! There's a time and a place! Arghhh! ...*Spara la magia per mirare... Purificare!* And! *Purificare!*"

Wise chain cast. Twin glimmering lights of purification shot down the hall.

The light enveloped the skeletons, and they vanished in the blink of an eye, all forcibly sent to the afterlife.

The monsters were defeated!

"Mwa-ha-ha! This is my true power! 'Wise, you're amazing!' 'Wise, you're such a beautiful Mage!' Go on, tell me more!"

After that impressive display, the children showered Wise with praise:

"Wahhh! Monsters! I'm scaaared!"

"Mommyyy! Moooooommyyyyy! Wahhhhh!"

"Hey, why are the kids all crying?!"

"I-it's okay! The monsters are gone! …Wise! This is the real struggle! Our fight has just begun!"

"I—I know! Let's do this!"

A group of sobbing children appeared. What now?

Wise attacked.

"Um, um… L-looky here! I'm a fluffy bunny, hop, hop, hop! Don't cry, everybunny! Let's all hop together!" *Hop, hop!*

At her age, acting like this was still inherently mortifying, but she cast aside her pride, summoning her cutest voice and body language!

The sobbing children stopped crying, staring at Wise.

"Wahhh! She's trying to distract us!"

"It's so obviously forced! Wahhhh!"

"You're awfully perceptive children! Who taught you those words?!"

"Sheesh, I should have known Wise wasn't up to the task… Very well. Leave this to me."

Medhi attacked.

"Hey, kids, you don't need to cry. I'm here with you. I'm only thinking of you. I'm really, really nice like that."

Medhi smiled like the holy mother herself!

The sobbing children stopped crying and stared at her.

"Wahhh, that's really creepy!"

"She's definitely hiding her true personality! Wahhh!"

"No!! No, I'm not! What you see is what you get with me!"

"These kids are so sharp; they instantly see your rotten core! …But we aren't getting anywhere at this rate, so… Right, raw power it is!"

Morals be damned, Wise was ready to solve this problem with magic…

…But first…

The sobbing children attacked!

"*Sniff, sniff*… Um, lady? Um, um… I need to go potty…"

"Huh? Potty? …Oh, right, the bathroom… Not really any around here…" said Wise.

"I need to go, too!"

"You too?" asked Medhi. "...Wh-what should we do? I suppose we could head back to that room... No, the casino toilets might be closer..."

"I want a snack! Wahhh!"

"A snack? H-hold on, lemme solve the toilet problem first..."

"Ah! I just saw something moving! I'll go look!"

"W-w-w-wait!! Don't go off alone!" shouted Medhi.

They tried to give chase, but... "I gotta pee *now!*" "Whaa—?!" "Um... Over here?" And while they were helping with that, "Hey, hey, where are the snacks?" "Wait just a minute on those!" The situation was only getting worse. "Oh! I saw something!" "Something over there, too!" "Don't wander off!" They were scattering in all directions, the children's innocent chain attacks erupting all around them.

""...I just can't deal...with kids...""

Wise and Medhi's energy reserves ran out.

GAME OVER...

They were never heard from again...

Obviously joking.

"A-anyway, there's bathrooms upstairs, and they have snacks and loads of games! So please, listen to us!"

"We're almost there! Come on, I'm begging you. We're seriously going to start crying soon. Give us a break!"

""""Okay, fiiine, I guess. If we gotta...""""

"Ack... Such condescension... Little brats..."

"Right, everyone hold hands! Don't let go!"

Wise took the lead and Medhi took the rear, the children all grouped between them.

All aboard the bunny train! "Let's go! Chugga-chugga..." "I thought bunnies went hop, hop?" "Yeah, they hop!" "Argh... H-hop...hop!" They pressed onward, embarrassing sound effects included.

Wise and Medhi were thoroughly exhausted—physically and mentally.

"*Sigh...* Dealing with children is seriously draining... It's so much easier to fight monsters..." said Wise.

"You are so right…" replied Medhi. "Mothers with small children have to do this every day, don't they? …Did I wear my mother out like this, I wonder?"

"For real. My mom's an awful person, but even she managed to look after me when I was really little… I feel like I'm actually starting to respect her… Uh… Huh?"

A figure appeared in the hall in front of them. Another monster?

No, an elderly man in a black suit—the casino's assistant manager.

"Wise, Medhi, well done. It seems you've successfully rescued the children. Splendid."

"Thanks for coming to meet us. Of course, we could handle this."

"The information you provided was invaluable. Thank you so much."

"Not at all. I should be thanking you. I'll take the children from here." The assistant manager turned to the hall behind him. "If you would be so kind?"

A group of Bunny Girls came forward, securing the children. "Bye-bye, ladies!" "Let's play again!" "Um, okay…" "If we get the chance…" They couldn't very well say "never again," but it was clearly written on their faces.

"My, my. Were they a bit much for you?"

"W-well, I mean, it just kinda felt a bit too soon for us, you know?"

"Y-yes… We're a long way from having any of our own."

"All the more reason to gain experience where you can. I recommend proactively pursuing any quests that will allow you to develop your maternal skills."

"Ughhh… I'm soooo done with these day-care quests…"

"I believe only Masato should have to suffer where maternal things are concerned. We've had quite enough."

"Now, don't say that! I mean this for your own good… But that aside, first we must resolve the matter at hand."

"Mm. Right. That."

"Yes. Let us do what needs be done."

The children were safely with the staff. Rescue mission: complete.

Their next mission was to assist Mamako and Shiraaase in the arena. Wise and Medhi nodded at each other and ran off in that direction…

…but before they did, the assistant manager stopped them.

"Oh, sorry. I know you're in a hurry, but if you could spare a moment? There's something I forgot to mention earlier."

"Yeah? What?"

"The arena down below has a rather unusual functionality installed."

"Unusual how?"

"One that will catch Sorella off guard and allow us to turn the tables and resolve this situation, guaranteeing a happy ending... In short..."

...it'll be more fun to see it in action.

And now, back to the Alzare recovery team.

Not much of a team, though—it was just Masato.

"Entrusted with a vital task, throwing myself into solitary conflict... Heh... At last, I'm finally a hero!"

He was alone but thoroughly enjoying himself. He hadn't been this excited in a while.

He was running down a corridor, the map Medhi had given him in one hand.

A group of skeletons blocked his path.

"Kah⁄kah⁄kah... Living one... Soon you will wander here for all eternity as we do..."

"You're talking to me, right? Not to anyone else? You're treating me, personally, as your enemy? Just me? You're sure?"

"Huh? Y⁄yes, you! Tremble in fear as—"

"Ohhhh, this is great! I'm being targeted! Not Mom, not anyone else! Me! This is amazing! Hell yeah!"

"Huh? Why is he so happy?"

Thinking about it, Masato was pretty sure this had never happened before.

Mamako was always at the front of the party. Even the Four Heavenly Kings reserved all their aggro for her and never even glanced at Masato, the ostensible hero. That was just his life here.

But not now! For once, I'm actually the star!

He was overjoyed.

"Ohhhhh! Yeah! Identity Establishment Slaaaaash!"

"Eeeeeeek?!"

An improvised attack name, kinda crappy, but whatever.

Spraying tears of joy, Masato sliced his way through the skeletons.

The Holy Sword in his hand, Firmamento, was specialized in fighting flying enemies and generally not the best against surface foes.

But that didn't matter now! Infused with the power of his joy, it was supereffective against the negative energy of the undead monsters! Extra fun!

"More! More! Bring it on! Keep 'em comiiiing! Ha-ha!"

"What's wrong with this kid?! He's terrifying!"

"Let me fight mooooore! This is my big momeeeent!"

Masato mercilessly kicked terrified skeletons out of his way. "I found more!" **"He's after uuuus!"** A ghost tried to turn invisible and flee, but he cut it down, too! Joyous slaughter!

"So much fun! I've never had this much fun in my life! Too much fun! I'm so glad I lived to see this daaaaay!!"

"If I'd known I was going to be this scared, I'd rather not have died and come back as a monsterrrr!!"

Monsters tried to pretend not to see him and run away, but he caught and defeated them, too! Never even glancing at the heaps of gems they left behind, Masato ran on!

After a while:

"Ha-ha-ha-haaaa... Oh... Look, a suspicious door!"

A stone door stood in the passage ahead. There were even carvings on it, clearly marking it as a place of importance.

He checked his map, and it was, in fact, where the Alzare was.

"Sheesh, already at the end point... I kinda wanna rerun that last path like ten more times, but I've got to complete my mission here and get back to the arena."

Resisting temptation, Masato reached for the door. "If it won't open, maybe then I'll go back..." But the door opened easily. Too bad.

Inside was a wide-open space with dull stone walls and rows of ancient metal candlesticks.

As Masato stepped inside, the candles lit up, one by one...revealing a kingly figure at the back.

"Ho-ho... To come this far alone... I admire your courage, at least."

The candlelight revealed a Gold Knight Skeleton, clad in golden armor.

"…I assume you're the room guardian, then?"

"**That I am! I am the protector of that which lies within this room, the treasure known as Alzare.**"

"Cool, then this is the right place… Shall we?"

"**Very well. Put your life on the line, and you may just stand a chance, brave boy.**"

The Gold Knight Skeleton had a shield in its left hand and a sword in its right. It gave a knight's salute and made ready to battle.

Masato raised his sword…but the tip was shaking.

"**What's wrong? Lost your nerve, boy?**"

"N-no, that's not it…"

"**Then why are you trembling?**"

"Obviously, 'cause I'm just so happy! I'm so happy I could cry!"

"**Huh?**"

"I've been waiting for a moment like this! My chance to shine! To get called stuff like, 'brave boy,' to have one-on-one fights like this! This is the adventure I've wanted all along! So that's why I'm just so incredibly happy… Nng!"

The tears were blurring his vision. His nose was running. It was all hanging out.

"**I-if you're blubbering like that…you must have really been suffering…**"

"I have! My tale is one of tears and woe!"

"**I see… Hmm… I suppose I could listen to your story…**"

"You will? Then let me tell you!"

"**Hmm… Very well… But only after you die and become one of my minions!**"

An instant later the Gold Knight Skeleton had closed the gap between them, swinging his ancient sword.

It was a blow designed to split his head in two, but Masato raised Firmamento, blocking it and letting it slide down the blade. He managed to jump backward, recovering.

"Whoa! You don't hold back, huh?"

"**This is a fight to the death! Why would I hold back?**"

"Exactly! That's what I'm talkin' about!"

His howl blasted away the momentary chill, and then Masato attacked, giving as good as he got.

Masato lunged directly toward the Gold Knight Skeleton...but that was a feint, and he took a quick step to the right, swinging. "Hah!" His blow was caught by the shield, but...

...he soon swung again. Using the momentum of the sword's recoil to spin and swing from the other direction...

"Your counter is too slow!"

"What...?!"

...the Gold Knight Skeleton thrust his shield forward.

The shield released an unnatural light. This was...!

Tch! *I dunno what that is, but I shouldn't soak it head-on!*

Masato quickly canceled his attack and thrust out his left arm.

He'd intended to deploy his shield wall, but the moment the enemy shield struck it, Masato's arm jerked back with a sudden pain.

"Unh?! My shoulder...!"

"Don't worry, that pain won't last long... I'll end it for you!"

"Death wasn't the kind of painkiller I had in mind! Hah!"

An upward slash aimed at his throat, deflected by a mighty downswing.

Masato quickly backed away from the Gold Knight Skeleton, putting space between them.

Crap... My left arm's so numb I can't move it...

That shield's attack must have had some sort of stun effect, preventing him from acting. He may have avoided a direct hit but had been unable to completely negate it.

He held his sword in his right hand, his left arm hanging limp. Masato's defense was sealed.

His expression remained confident, but there was definitely a sweat on his brow.

Dammit! Time will cure this stun effect... I've got to hold out until then!

Masato slid his feet backward, slowly increasing the distance, trying to buy some time.

It wasn't working.

"This fight is over! Ready? Here I coooome!"

"What the...?! You're fast!"

The Gold Knight Skeleton was already right in front of him, committed to a fatal blow. Masato had been focused on buying time and was too late to block the blow with his blade. At this rate...!

But just before the blade sank into Masato's shoulder, it froze.

"Huh...?"

He didn't know why it had stopped. The skeleton's bony face offered no clues.

But this was his chance.

He gave everything he had, swinging his sword frantically.

"Rahhhhhhhhhhhhhhhhhh!"

Firmamento let loose a powerful swing.

The transparent sword snapped the ancient blade in two and cut the Gold Knight Skeleton's head clean off its shoulders.

"Ah-ha! *Hahhh... Hahhh.........* Yessss!"

All the air in his lungs and fear in his heart came rushing out at once, and Masato crowed with victory.

The Gold Knight Skeleton's head rolled next to him.

"Phooey. My head came off!"

"Holy crap?! You can still talk?! ...W-wait, you're not gonna revive, are you...?"

"Fear not. I am defeated and will soon fade... Enjoy your victory, boy. You may take the Alzare."

"...Cool, I'll do that."

The fight was over. Masato put Firmamento back in its scabbard and headed toward the back of the room.

There was a pedestal made out like an altar and a small treasure box on it.

On the lookout for traps, he opened it...and found a single book inside.

"Is this Alzare...?"

It didn't have a title anywhere. He opened it and found it crammed full of lines of ASCII code. "Ah, this has gotta be it." Alzare, the program used to mess with the NPC configuration, had been turned into an item. That had to be the case here.

At least turn it into hieroglyphs or something! Anything that would fit the setting! But there was time to gripe about that later.

What mattered was that he'd achieved his goal.

"I did it... By my own hand... My own power alone... I finally did it... Yes, if I put my mind to it, I can succeed! I'm aaaaaaaaawesoooooome!"

His party wasn't with him. There was nobody around to hear.

So Masato totally let himself cut loose, shouting things he'd normally never let himself say. **"Ah, youth."** "You're still here?!" Being overheard by a Gold Knight Skeleton was so mortifying he nearly died on the spot.

Masato turned to leave or maybe run away... But first:

"...Um, can I ask a question? Why'd you stop your swing back there? Was there a reason for that?"

If the Gold Knight Skeleton's sword had followed through, Masato would have lost. His opponent should have won.

As it faded, the skull replied, **"It was the shirt you wear, boy."**

"My shirt? ...This is just something my mom bought for me when we were out shopping... What about it?"

"A gift from your mother? That explains it... In that moment, I sensed powerful emotions emanating from your shirt. It unleashed an intense protective power...strong enough to block my blow."

Masato's shirt had been given the power to negate a single attack of any type thanks to his mother's special skill, A Mother's Love Enhancement.

When purchasing the shirt, Mamako had hugged it tight, making a wish upon it.

"Did you not see it, boy? I suppose not. They say no child ever knows just how dear he is to his parents... You should thank your mother later."

And with that, the Gold Knight Skeleton vanished for good.

"...Geez... Once again, it was all thanks to Mom..."

The tears flowed freely, and he couldn't see a thing. He was forced to stand still for a time.

*   *   *

Masato left the room and hurried toward the arena, making smooth progress. He knew the way now, and all the monsters shrieked and fled when they saw him.

He was rather upset.

"Anyway, I recovered the Alzare! Wise and Medhi will have delivered the kids and be on their way back, too! So I gotta get back there first... and this time, *this time*, I swear, I'll get to show my power! Somehow! Argh!"

Tears trailed behind him as he ran.

He soon found himself before a familiar arch. Beyond that lay the arena.

Masato drew Firmamento and, with the wind at his back, rushed in.

"Please! I begging! Give me a chance to shine...! Uh, wait... Something's wrong... Why is the wind...? Whoaaa?!"

He suddenly felt like he was floating and quickly stopped in his tracks. He'd thought there was a wind at his back but it now felt like he was being sucked toward the gate.

He looked ahead and saw a tornado centered on the stage. Stones the size of casino chips, all caught up in the winds...

...No, wait. The stone chips were the ones generating the tornado.

"Yo! What is this? The heck's going on? ...Argh, is there nobody here? Porta? Shiraaase? ...Mom?"

"Oh! I hear Masato! Masato's here!"

"That you, Porta? Where...? Oh, I see you! And Shiraaase!"

Some distance from the tornado was a coffin, and Porta was curled up behind it.

Masato ran over to her.

"Well, at least you're safe! Good!"

"Yes! I'm fine! Ms. Shiraaase is dead again, but that's kept me out of harm's way!"

"'Cause death invalidates all attacks, right? Thanks a ton, Shiraaase!"

He felt like the back of the coffin was proudly saying, "You're welcome." It seemed quite satisfied with itself. He would leave it in charge of protecting Porta.

Masato hid behind it as well, taking stock again.

A tornado in the center of the arena. Mothers in the stands, huddled with one another against the winds. Like a natural disaster unfolding.

"So what's up with the tornado? ...And where's Mom?"

"W-well..."

"I can fill you in theeere," a languid voice carried over the wind.

Sorella. She was sitting on a tatami-sized giant magic tome, which was floating on the wind.

"Where should I staaart? Hmmm... Hmmm..."

"Keep it snappy! Bullet points only!"

"Then I wiiiill. Mamako and I are fighting right nooow. Mamako said she was going to lecture meeee, and that sounded so duuull, so I decided to defeat heeer."

"Okay, okay, so?"

"Theeeen... Once I wiiin, I'm going to make it so that Mamakoooo and all the moms in the staaands aren't mothers anymoooore. Won't that be fuuun?"

"They won't be mothers? What the heck does that mean? ...Whatever, not like Mom'll lose this fight. A happy end is inevitable."

"Mm... I'm not so suuure... I mean, look at the staaage. Seeeee? Mamako's really struuuuggling."

"Pfft, no way. Mom never struggles..."

He squinted, trying to see the stage through the tornado.

He could just barely see her standing on the stage, two swords equipped, swinging them over and over...

...yet the tornado around her just kept on swirling.

"Th-that's not right... If Mom's attacking...like, more things should be happening... Can she not break through the tornado?"

"That's riiight. Mamako can't do a thing about iiit! How straaange! The secreeeet...is right heeere!"

Sorella pulled a single stone chip out of her pocket and tossed it to Masato.

He reflexively caught it, but a moment later, it flew away. "Wha—? Aughh?!" It struck him on the chin, then flew away, joining the tornado.

"Wh-what was that? It moved on its own? And hit me?!"

"Of course it diiid! It's a monsteeer! Made from old chips they used in this areeena, an undead monster powered by the regrets of losers who ruined their lives heeeere... Hmm... With all of them in the tornadoooo...there's, like, a million of theeem."

"A million... A m-million monsters?!"

"That's riiiight. And Mamako's attaaaacks...they split the damage evenlyyyy. Sooo...even if she did a million points of damage with each attaaaack...against a million enemiiiies..."

Her two attacks would only do two points of damage to each individual enemy.

"*Tch*, that explains it."

"It dooooes. Mwa-haaa. This means I wiiiin."

Mamako's overwhelming firepower was at a disadvantage against overwhelming numbers. She couldn't cut through them.

And the moment she slowed her attacks, they'd all attack, and she might well lose.

The mothers in the stands were clutching their heads, fearing the worst.

Gazing at them, Sorella inhaled a lungful of the mothers' collective despair, smiling with immense pleasure.

But...

"To hell with that! This isn't over yet! ...There's no way my mother will ever lose! After all, she's my mom!"

Masato let his feelings spill out.

"Ohhh? Are you going to butt iiin? ...Hmmm... Fiiiine. You helping her out won't change a thiiing. Suit yourseeelf. I'll allow iiiit."

"Well, thanks! I'll make you regret underestimating me!"

This wasn't a bluff. Masato was sure.

After all, the chip monsters were *flying*.

"This is my chance to shine! Leave flying enemies to meeeeee!"

Firmamento, the Holy Sword of the Heavens, was about to demonstrate its true potential.

He pulled and swung the transparent blade, and it fired a crescent-shaped light beam that rocketed toward the tornado with such force it seemed certain to cut it in half.

"Goooooooooooo!"

The beam hit one of the old chips at the edge of the tornado!

And as it did, the beam dissipated.

"...Mm?"

Masato defeated an old chip!

Freed of regrets, the old chip became an antique chip and fell to the ground at Masato's feet! He got a drop item!

That was cool and all but not the point.

"Ah, right... My attacks are single target..."

"No matter how big the effect iiiis, you can only hit oooone. Such a shaaaame! Have fuuun!"

"Arghhh... I-in that case I just have to attack another 999,999 times, right?! Fine! I'm gonna do it! Damn it alllllllll!"

Masato attacked! Only 999,998 to go!

Five minutes later.

"...S-so...tired..."

His arms shaking from overexertion, Masato examined the results of his efforts.

At his feet lay around one hundred chips.

Inside the tornado, Mamako was still battling furiously. She'd seen Masato and glanced his way occasionally but was much too busy fighting. He had to do something soon, but...

"Th-this isn't right... This isn't all I'm capable of... I'm not just here to let Mom spoil me... I'm capable...!"

"And yetttt...you seem really tired and ready to give uuup. Masatooo... *Capable* isn't the word you're looking fooor."

"Th-that's not true! See? I've already defeated a hundred!"

"Trueeee... But a mere one hundred chips is a drop in the buckeeet. Completely poooointless."

"Maybe not!"

"A hundred is plenty!"

Masato recognized those voices.

"*Sigh*... Geez... You two sure took your time! Were you goofing off somewhere?"

Not wanting to admit how glad he was to see them, he settled for grumbling.

Wise and Medhi came running out of the passageway and stopped in front of Masato. They both hung their heads, the rabbit ears flopping forward.

"Yeah, about that... Those little twerps..." *Slump.*

"It was just awful... Children are so..." *Sulk.*

"R-right, not goofing off. Mortal peril, got it. Good job... But, uh, let's leave the catching up for later! Look at this mess!"

"Yeah, this seems bad. There's a tornado and everything! Super-gaudy."

"Is that Mamako fighting in there? Good! She's in just the right place."

The two girls seemed both aware of the significance of the situation and yet were weirdly enjoying themselves.

"Wahhh, wahhh. Don't bother pretending you're still confideeent. Besiiiides, Wise and Medhi are my staaaaff... Go back to the casino and do your jooobs."

"Hate to break it to yaaa, but we paid off our deeeeeeeebts. We don't work for you anymooooooooooore... Alsooooooooooo..."

"Those children you locked uuuuuup? We freed them aaaaaall!"

"Mmm?! Well, that was unnecessaryyyyy! Now I'm peeeeeved! ...Alsooo, why are you talking like thaaat? Take this conversation seriouslyyy!"

"Uh, we're just talking like you do."

"I don't sound anything like that, stuuuupid. Besiiides..."

"Yeah, whatever. We're done mimicking it, don't worry."

"Also, we'd like to introduce you to a special function of this arena!"

Medhi picked up one of the old chips from the floor at her feet and flicked it aloft with her thumb. The chip dissipated in midair.

An instant later, the arena grew darker, and the sound of a drumroll immediately followed.

Then a magic stone came flying in, glowing like a spotlight, and began orbiting over the mothers in the stands, around and around the circular arena.

"Wh-what the...?"

"Isn't it obvious? It's drawing a winner," said Wise.

"And the winner is… Over there."

The magic stone stopped, illuminating a single mother. But she just looked around, unsure why she was being lit up.

"Yep, that mother's the winner! Congrats! Now…"

"Everyone, eyes to the stage!"

Following the two Bunny Girls' instructions, Masato, Sorella, Porta (from her hiding place behind the coffin), and the mothers in the crowd all looked to the stage.

Then light shot out of the stage, forming letters so bright they were visible through the tornado:

Status Up! Target: Mother

And there you have it.

"Um… Wise, Medhi… Explain."

"Sure, sure, got it… The assistant manager told us this trick," explained Wise. "This arena has a roulette function on it, a bonus for the people fighting on the stage. A random buff."

"If you defeat one of the old chips that spawn here and use them, you can activate the roulette, and it'll select a single person from the stands," added Medhi.

"And everyone who shares the same job as that chosen person gets a huge ability buff."

"So if there's a swordsman fighting in the ring, and a swordsman in the audience gets picked, then the swordsman who's fighting will get a huge status boost, too. If a person with some other job gets picked, that's a miss, and the boost doesn't activate."

And thus, the Bunny Girls' arena roulette tutorial concluded.

So now…

"That's the first I've heard of thiiis… S-soooo…since the audience is made up of the mothers I brought heeere—and they're all motheeeers—and Mamako is onstaaage…and she's a motheeer… Th-th-th…that meeeans… Aughhhhh!"

Sorella started to panic, but it was already too late.

This was way beyond her previous spoiling.

Time to spin the arena roulette 100 percent guaranteed to buff Mamako only!

"Okay, let's do this!" Medhi yelled.

"Spin that roulette round and round!" cried Wise.

"I'll handle keeping Sorella at bay. The two of you kill more chips! ...Porta, you gather the chips and use them!"

"Okay! Leave it to me!"

"R-right, let's do this..." Masato said, belatedly trying to take charge.

"Um! Please let me help, too!" said one mother. She came running toward them with a glowing flyswatter in her hand.

"Um, and this mother is... Wait, what's with that weird blinding flyswatter...?"

"She's the mother from the general store! Mama gave her motherly powers, and they fought together! All the mothers did!"

Porta pointed toward the stands, where the mothers were all brandishing glowing rolled-up flyers, despite the raging winds.

"Whoa, you guys are fired up. I can feel that mother power from here... Are those rolled-up flyers? You'd think they could at least be transformed into some sort of holy weapon-like thing... Whatever! The more people help, the better!"

"W-w-w-wait, wait, waiiiit!! Please, seriously, just waaaait!!"

They did not wait.

The chip contingent swiftly began knocking them out of the sky.

Masato and Wise were up first.

"You've got magic so you can take on a whole bunch, but I've only got single-target attacks! Bear that in mind and give me a handicap, okay?"

"I refuse!"

"Wow, such a manly Bunny Girl..."

"You've already scored a hundred chips, Masato! And I'm gonna pass you in no time! ...*Spara la magia per mirare... Luce Sparo!* And! *Luce Sparo!*"

Wise's chain cast activated. Light bullets with purifying powers shot toward the chip tornado.

Over a thousand bullets of light instantly rocketed her score ahead of Masato's...!

"I upped the bullet count! This way I'll easily... Uh, wait..."

Nope. She got too greedy and split the power, making each bullet too weak to take anything down.

Old chips in critical condition came fluttering in Masato's direction. "Oh, nice!" He took them out. Easy-peasy! "Those were mine!" Wise started stomping them to death.

But someone else was doing better than either of them.

"We can't lose to these children! Come on!"

"They're just like the insects that invade our homes and frighten our children!"

"We're all mothers here! Time to show a mother's true strength!"

The mothers in the stands were going wild. Flyswatters and rolled-up flyers going *thwack, thwack, thwack*, chip after chip falling to the ground. It was nuts.

"...Moms can be amazing sometimes," said Masato.

"They've got that bug-swatting motion down pat. It's kinda impressive, in its own way. Like, they look seriously reliable suddenly? But we can't let them win!"

"Oh, right! I've got to demonstrate the hero's power!"

Wise and Masato shook off their awe and set to work.

Around their competition, a game of tag was starting.

"Hngggg... Wh wh-wh-what noooow?! I could stack my debuff skiiiill... Oh, I caaan't! Because I'm controlling a million monsterrrrs! I don't have enough power left for that skiiill!"

"So will you release your control of the old chips?" *Grin.*

"I can't do thaaat! Mamako would get freeeee! ...I'm top class when it comes to my debuff skiiill and undead control aaaarts but I've got no HP or defeeeense! I'm just a normal magic joooob! I can't fight her directlyyyy!"

"Then what shall you do?" *Grin.*

"W-weeeell... I definitely think I should run away from you, Medhiii! The way you smile without smiling is really creeeepy!"

Sorella made the right judgment call.

Dark power was erupting from Medhi's high-cut leotard, painting her normally beautiful smile black.

"You see, I've got a lot of pent-up frustration here... I'm not trying to be perfect all the time anymore, see? But my mother's teachings are ingrained in me now... So everything that's happened since we hit the casino has been sooo stressful..."

"A-about thaaat! I'm s-s-s-sorryyy! I'm sorry I used my skill to make you looooose! But, buuuut...you paid the debt baaack! Aren't we eveeeen?!"

"I may have paid off the debt, but that didn't cancel out the rage building within me! Arghhh, I really need to hit something! Is there nothing around here worth kicking? ...I've got to dispel this fury somehow..."

"Th-there's a wall right over theeere!! It looks ripe for kickiiing!"

"Oh, there you are." *Grin.*

"She's looking right at meeeee!!"

Sorella slipped down off her giant magic tome and began moving at the highest speed her languorous body could manage... Swinging her staff and kicking the air, Medhi was slowly gaining on her.

And:

"We've collected a whole bunch of chips! Porta, they're yours!"

"Leave it to me! I'll use them! ...Will it win? It'll win! *Hyah!*"

Porta tossed the chip, spinning the arena roulette.

The room went dark and the selection process began. The magic stone roamed the crowd, and the spotlight landed on... "Oh, gosh! Me?" ...Naturally, another mother.

Status Up! Target: Mother

Again.

"Porta, here's another!"

"Got it! Will it win? It'll win! *Hyah!*"

And again, "What? Me, this time?" The roulette picked a mother.

Status Up! Target: Mother

And again.

"I've brought these from the stands! Can you take care of 'em?"

"Of course! I won't waste the mothers' efforts! *Hyah!*"

Porta quickly tossed the new chips! On we go! **Status Up! Target: Mother.** More! **Status Up! Target: Mother.** Even more!

So many announcements were made...that the time at last arrived.

"! ...Here it comes!"

"What d'you mean, Masato?"

"Our OP party member's OP attack! …Wise! Medhi! Get away from the stage! Porta, back behind that coffin!"

How did Masato sense it coming?

Because she was his mother. He just *knew*.

"Everybody down!"

A moment later:

The tornado and the chips within it swelled and burst.

A million chips came raining down on the stage, revealing a mother beyond compare. You-know-who.

"Whew… That all worked out somehow! Thank goodness."

Mamako smiled, wiping the sweat from her brow.

Then her gaze locked onto Masato. She knew instantly where her beloved son was.

"Ma-kun, you're safe! You all are!"

"Yeah, thanks… You had it pretty rough, too, huh?"

"I did! I'm every bit as tired as I am after spring cleaning!"

"I can't really relate to that kind of exhaustion."

"But now that I've seen your face, all my exhaustion just went away! I think I could clean another ten houses! Hee-hee!"

"Yeah, again, never cleaned a house, can't relate… *Sigh*… Doesn't matter… So… I think it's time this mom casino shut down."

Masato glanced at Medhi. She appeared to have transformed into a (dark) Bunny Girl, but she still caught his drift.

She put just a little more pressure on Sorella, driving her up onto the stage.

"*Hahhh…hahhh*… S-stoppp! Stop chasing meee! Uh… W-waiiiit?! Mamakoooo?!"

"That's right… Sorella, we need to talk."

"No, we doooon't! I didn't do anything wroooong! I just altered the way the NPC mothers and children thiiiink… Experimented with how they'd aaact… Then gathered them here so I could laugh at theeem!"

"Guilty," said Masato.

"Alsoooo… I used my debuff skiiiill…so that nobody could ever win at my casinooo…"

"The assistant manager told us, but that's super-obnoxious. Guilty!" said Wise.

"Definitely guilty. This shall not stand." Medhi's aura growled ominously.

"Also, uuum... I suppoooose...I did turn people who had debts into priiizes..."

"That's really naughty!" piped up Porta.

The four jurors delivered a guilty verdict.

Time for sentencing.

"Mom, if you want to give her a lecture, I won't stop you. But I think you need to give her a good scolding first or she won't listen."

"You think? ...I suppose I should scold her properly first."

Mamako held up an index finger.

"Gahhhhh?! W-w-w-waiiiitt!! Mamako's scoldings even did in Amanteeeee!"

"Oh yeah, they did. She could reflect all attacks and had crazy strength and endurance, but one scolding and she was at death's door."

"I can't, I can't, I can't, I caaaan't! I'll never surviiive! I'm a magic claaaass! I've got no enduraaaance! And Mamako's really, really, really buffed up right nowwww! You shouldn't bully the weeeak!"

"That's true. And, well...you seem quite frightened, Sorella. Making children listen because they're scared is the wrong way to scold... It's best if you listen willingly, understand what I'm trying to say, and appreciate the earnestness of my request. So..."

Mamako sat down in front of Sorella, putting her eyes on the same level.

"Okay?"

A big smile and a gentle, "Okay?"

In that moment, everyone present felt the world change.

The arena had been brimming with bloodthirst, but now it was like a meadow bathed in sunlight. A pleasant breeze brushed by, and birds sang. The perfect place for a chat.

"Okay?"

This was Mamako's wish. And some supernatural power with

control over space itself had altered their surroundings to allow that wish to be granted.

As a result: "Okay, I'm listening." "Totally!" "What is it?" "I want to listen, Mama!" Even the party members Mamako wasn't addressing gathered around her, sitting beside her, joining the conversation as if it was the most natural thing in the world. Even the coffin!

And, "Oh, a chat?" "I'm all ears." "Me too." Mothers began filing out of the stands and sitting down around Mamako.

As if that weren't enough, **"What are we talking about?" "Can we listen?"** Undead monsters began filing out of the ruins, gathering around.

Sorella had stubbornly rejected the idea, but even she—

"Huhhhh? You're all listeniiing? Umm... Then I guess I couuuld... l-listen to...what M-M-M-Mamakooooo... Noooooooooot!"

—stopped herself in the nick of time.

She banged her head on the stage several times, trying to clear her mind.

"I'm one of the Four Heavenly Kings of the Libere Rebelliooon! Look, I admit you nearly had me for a second theeere! But I won't give in to your weird poweeers!"

"Oh dear. Then whatever shall we do?"

"You'll do nothiiing! This is all overrr! ...Oh, I knooow!"

Sorella picked up an old chip from her feet.

"Mamakooo! Let's battle with thiiis! Toss this chiiip! If it's heads, you wiiiin. And tails, I wiiin. And if you win, I'll listen to what you have to saaay! ...But I have the ultimate debuff skill so victory will definitely be mine! Mwa-ha-haaa!"

Sorella's body glowed repeatedly, chain activating her skill. Trying to win but cratering Mamako's luck... But...

"Mm? Huh? No, wait, that's—"

"I won't waaait! Here goeees!"

Masato jumped up to stop her, but he was too late.

Sorella tossed the old chip.

And the arena roulette activated. "Huh?" "Uh-oh, she's done it now." The selection process began. The drumroll sounded, and the magic stone circled over the mothers' heads...

...and a moment later, the stone's spotlight locked onto Mamako. The light formed two letters:

JP

What?

"Ummmm... You, stunned-looking Bunny Giiiirl. Explaaain."

"Is this—?! I've heard the legends, but could it be?!"

"The fabled Jack-Mom-Pot?!"

"Uh, wait, Medhi... It just says JP. This is just a normal jackpot. No need to ram a mom in there."

Sorella hit the legendary jackpot! There was a thunderous fanfare, and the greatest prize in arena history was bestowed!

The old chips scattered around swirled up, suddenly turning into one ounce of gold before raining down on Sorella!

"I did iiiit! This means I wiiin! I'm making a fortuuuune! This is all miiiine! I acceeeept! Um... Huh? These gold coins are a little weeeird..."

A single coin plopped into Sorella's palm. It had an *S* on it. The next one had an *O*. Then came an *R*, and an *E*, an *L*, another *L*, and an *A*.

And after those: *D O N T M A K E F U N O F M O T H E R S*.

"D-does this meeean...? N-n-n-no waaay!! Aughhhhh?!"

Thanks to the "Okay?" effect, Mamako's message was being spelled out by the gold coins!

A single one-ounce gold coin was about an inch in diameter, with each weighing...well, one ounce. A million of those amount to...over thirty tons. A rain of extremely heavy words swiftly buried Sorella completely.

"Oh dear! We'd better rescue her!" Mamako cried, turning white as a sheet.

"No, it's too late... This is gold... She's been crushed..."

Masato put his palms together. RIP.

"Wait! I thought I saw something really fast slide under the gold!" Porta shouted. Always eagled-eyed.

A second later:

The mountain of gold erupted, like something exploded within.

As the coins scattered, they revealed...Amante, with Sorella tucked under her arm.

"Yep, my reflection skill's the best. It's particularly powerful against the forces of physics."

"You reflected a mountain of gold coins? Dang... Wait, why are you here?!"

"That would be telling. Look, she is one of the Four Heavenly Kings, nominally, so I figured I should at least collect her. In return, I grant these gold coins to the heroes who defeated Sorella... I think you get a bigger reward than I do, which is very irritating, but..."

She glanced down at the casino flyer, frowning.

Regardless, Amante slung Sorella over a shoulder, intact but unconscious, and ran away.

"Oh, thank goodness! I'm so glad Sorella's all right." *Whew.*

"Yo, Mom! This is no time to be acting all relieved! They're getting away!"

It was all over in an instant.

C H U T E S AND M O T H E R S

5

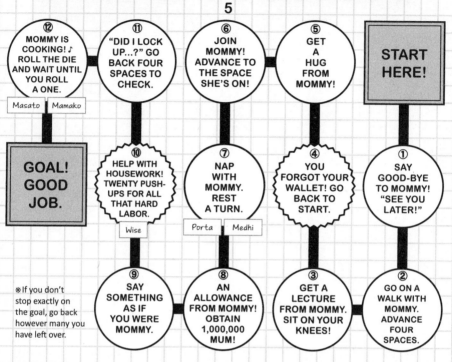

⑫ MOMMY IS COOKING! ♪ ROLL THE DIE AND WAIT UNTIL YOU ROLL A ONE.

Masato | Mamako

⑪ "DID I LOCK UP...?" GO BACK FOUR SPACES TO CHECK.

⑥ JOIN MOMMY! ADVANCE TO THE SPACE SHE'S ON!

⑤ GET A HUG FROM MOMMY!

START HERE!

GOAL! GOOD JOB.

⑩ HELP WITH HOUSEWORK! TWENTY PUSH-UPS FOR ALL THAT HARD LABOR.

Wise

⑦ NAP WITH MOMMY. REST A TURN.

Porta | Medhi

④ YOU FORGOT YOUR WALLET! GO BACK TO START.

① SAY GOOD-BYE TO MOMMY! "SEE YOU LATER!"

※ If you don't stop exactly on the goal, go back however many you have left over.

⑨ SAY SOMETHING AS IF YOU WERE MOMMY.

⑧ AN ALLOWANCE FROM MOMMY! OBTAIN 1,000,000 MUM!

③ GET A LECTURE FROM MOMMY. SIT ON YOUR KNEES!

② GO ON A WALK WITH MOMMY. ADVANCE FOUR SPACES.

 Everyone but Medhi's got a chance at the goal this turn...

 Wise. Please roll a six.

 I will not! Ha! Wait, a six?! Three forward, three back, and... Oh boy, more push-ups!

 I got a five! Waiting for Mama's cooking!

 Right... I'm gonna roll a one and win this thing! I'm betting everything on it! Here goes! ...Three...

 Then it's Mommy's turn! Oh, a one! My, my, I've reached the goal!

 ...Yeah...I knew that'd happen...

Epilogue

Once they escaped the ancient ruins, the mothers never even glanced at the row of casinos. They headed straight to the residential areas where their families and children were at home waiting for them. Each had battles lying ahead of them to reestablish themselves as mothers, but the core problem was resolved.

Shiraaase bid them farewell.

"Thank you for recovering Alzare. This is a huge help."

"You're welcome. I thought we'd need to readjust the mothers...but it kinda seems like they're taken care of."

"Yes. It seems they've remembered how it feels to be a mother, and I find myself wanting to see them conquer this issue through their own willpower. Now then... I'll be taking my leave. You've been a great help once again. Wish the assistant manager well for me."

And with that, she went away, the Alzare book in hand.

Masato's party went to see the assistant manager. They figured he deserved a report, at least. He welcomed them with a warm smile.

"Well done, everyone. Sounds like you had quite the time of it."

"Yeah, thanks. Once we put our minds to it...I always save the day," Masato boasted.

"Masato always does great! You're so cool!"

"Hee-hee. Yes, he is! Ma-kun always comes through."

"R-right... Yeah... Th-that's...what I've always dreamed of..."

Masato went off to cry.

Wise spoke up next, sounding a little annoyed.

"So I guess this is a happy ending or whatever, but...I still got questions... Right, Medhi?"

"Indeed."

"You do? Like what, exactly?" asked Masato.

"Like who the assistant manager is!"

"He was up here yet seems to have been fully aware of everything that happened underground… Could we ask you to introduce yourself properly, sir?" Medhi asked with her beautiful smile.

The assistant manager returned a kindly old man smile and nodded.

"Very well," he said. "I shall reveal to you my true identity… I am the actual manager of this casino and the person in charge of the ancient ruins that sleep beneath the city."

"The actual manager… So Sorella stole your position from you?"

"She did. As for my race… Let me see… I suppose I should call myself a residual memory of the ancient people… To refer to myself as a god would be rather presumptuous, after all."

"Wha—? Y-you're a god?!"

"That is what my parameters say." He smiled.

"Why does everyone insist on clarifying that point?!"

"Ha-ha-ha, I do beg your pardon. At any rate, all you need to know is that I'm the manager of this casino… For a god, I am distinctly powerless."

His smiling face seemed rather forlorn.

The elderly assistant manager—or rather, the actual manager—turned toward Masato's party, speaking slowly.

"…Sorella showed up here quite recently. She strolled in like she had all the time in the world yet had everyone here under her control in the blink of an eye."

"She used Alzare to change your settings and those of the mothers and then did whatever she wanted?"

"NPCs like us are capable of independent thought. If unexpected changes interrupt our daily routines, we naturally sense that things have gone wrong. Sadly, we have no means of overriding our settings…"

"So you had no way of disobeying Sorella. Wow, she really sucks!" said Wise.

"However, salvation soon arrived. Someone strong, kind, sweet, warm, and with an aura as overwhelming as the earth or the ocean."

"That's gotta be Mamako," said Medhi.

"I think it's Mama, too!"

"Definitely our hero, Ma-kun!"

"Mom, please don't... Haven't I suffered enough...?"

"Ha-ha-ha! You're all correct! Masato is the source of Mamako's power. Believing that the hero and his mother would save us, I ushered you to this casino, like so."

Without even chanting a spell, the manager transformed into a small child.

A child dressed distinctively in some sort of old-fashioned ethnic garment.

"Hey, I've seen you before... Oh, right! The kid Mom and I were following!"

"Oh my! The child who snuck into the casino! It was the manager all along?"

"That is correct. I took the opportunity to guide you inside. Now, then..."

There was a puff of smoke, and he was back to normal.

"That's about all I have to share with you. Next, I'd like to discuss the payment owed to Mamako. If you wouldn't mind?"

"Payment to me? ...Whatever for?"

"The gold you earned for hitting the Jack-Mom-Pot in the underground casino."

"Please don't make that the official name. Let's just keep it a normal jackpot."

"Oh, right! You beat Sorella and got this mountain of gold!" said Wise.

"I believe the total value was well over a hundred billion. Possibly even getting close to a trillion," added Medhi.

"Uh...how many zeros are a trillion again?" asked Porta.

"A good deal of math is required to determine the exact value...but if I may be so bold as to offer a suggestion, I know just the thing to apply these funds to."

"You do?"

"Yes. I propose..." With the exact same smile, the manager looked Mamako directly in the eye. "...Mamako, I believe you hold a low opinion of gambling. In which case, why not use the money you won to buy all the casinos in Yomamaburg and shut them all down?"

"Shut the casinos down…?"

"Your actions have released the mothers from their gambling addiction and sent them home. However, there is every chance they will find their way back here again. To prevent relapses, you must eliminate the source. Isn't that the best way to handle these things? And the most effective way to prevent anyone else from falling victim to this addiction."

"But if we do that, won't everyone who works at the casinos be out of luck? I'm sure there are people just having fun, with proper restraint…"

"As you say. There will be people cast out, people angered by the loss of entertainment, and it will be an economic blow."

"Yes… Such a difficult decision…"

"Mamako, I want to know what decision you'll make on the matter. Please let me know your thoughts on the future of these casinos."

"Well…"

Everyone looked at her. Mamako thought for a good long time. And then she answered.

Yomamaburg, city of commerce.

The city's biggest attraction was, of course, the casinos. One sector of the city was a giant entertainment district, and one entire road was devoted to casinos, all with signs that read, NEWLY REMODELED!

Passersby were beckoned inside by men in black suits, bedazzled by the brilliant lights, dizzy with the prospect of fun housed within.

Saying a prayer, they exchanged cash for chips, sat down at the poker table, took a deep breath, and were ready to play.

Customers were blessed by the smile of a Bunny Girl (?), and as the match began…

"You there, you're betting a little high."

"What? Why is a Bunny Girl telling me what to— Uh, Mom?!"

"That's right! It's your mom! Look, Mom isn't about to tell you how to use the money you worked so hard to earn. But make sure you don't go too crazy now, okay?"

"R-right, I know… No, no, no, no! Why are you here, and dressed like a Bunny Girl?! Mom… As a Bunny Girl… I feel faint… Bleghhh…"

Surprises like this are part of the joy of a casino.

Drunk on the atmosphere, some Bunny Girls (?) forgot about their jobs and were playing the slots, but, well, that was part of the charm.

"Huh? What am I doing here...? ...And... Mom?! What are you doing?!"

"Huh? Oh my... I'm supposed to be working! I swore I would never gamble again, too...thank you. If you hadn't spoken to me, I might not have recovered my wits in time. I'd better get back to work!"

"R-right, glad I could do my duty as your son, but... Wait?! Why are you dressed like that?! It's so...immodest!"

Exchanging precious words with her son, receiving his support, the Bunny Girl (?) went hopping off to work some more.

Watching the staff at work, the manager smiled.

"Parents looking after children, children after parents, their bonds supporting one another, everyone having good, clean fun... Heh-heh... Brilliant, Mamako. Simply brilliant."

The casinos of Yomamaburg were booming, filled with noise and customers. Anyone was welcome within...

...well, at least in theory.

Masato's party put the casino behind them and set out.

Mamako seemed satisfied.

"Mothers feel safe if their children are with them and vice versa. A parent-child casino where bunny moms and children have fun together. Hee-hee... Isn't it lovely?"

Extremely satisfied.

The children less so.

"This is bad news... The manager made it so that all the casinos are using Mom's idea... If we don't escape now, the casino customers will catch us, and there'll be hell to pay..."

"If the children do anything crazy, their mothers are summoned in Bunny Girl clothes, and if the mothers do anything stupid, their children are summoned... There's no way anyone's gonna develop a gambling addiction this way," said Wise.

"And the cost of installing parent-child transport devices in all the casinos, as well as the mothers' part-time wages, all being paid for by Mamako's winnings... She just dumped the entire amount into it... I really feel like she should have kept a little for herself..." added Medhi.

"Mama's idea is amazing! They'll all be happy this way!"

Some broke out in a cold sweat, some just shook their heads, and Porta was thoroughly impressed... But either way, it was too late.

Time to move on.

"*Sigh*... Then I guess we're looking for a new adventure."

Basking in the breeze, Masato took a step forward, about to run away—

—when Mamako grabbed his arm. Of course.

"Hee-hee. Say, Ma-kun, didn't we make a lot of precious memories together? I had such a good time! Hee-hee!"

"Uh, sure, sure, glad to hear it."

"Wait, what? I think we need to hear more."

"I'd love to hear about it! What did Mama and Masato do together?!"

"Hee-hee, well, Ma-kun and I went on a date arm in arm, then we stopped at a lovely café, then I shampooed him, then we went shopping...and we studied how to let Mommy spoil him."

"These are all memories I'd rather forget."

"I think it sounds lovely," said Medhi. "So many wonderful things. May you never forget the events that transpired here. Heh-heh-heh."

"Geez, rub it in... Mm?"

Masato remembered something.

A whole lot of stuff had happened in Yomamaburg but first and foremost:

Wise and Medhi foisted Mom off on me so they could hit the casino...

And they'd fed Porta a bunch of crap to get her on board. Extra evil!

This wasn't something he should let stand.

"...Hey, Mom, got a second? I think you should probably say something about how Wise and Medhi tricked you into letting them go to the casino."

"Oh, that's right! I mean, part of that is Mommy's fault, but I should definitely scold the both of you."

Mamako's scolding... The one that started with "Tut, tut!" and ended with a laser death beam?!

Wise and Medhi both twitched, the blood draining from their faces.

"U-um... Medhi! Run for it!"

"Of course! ...Oh, Porta, you'd better come with!"

"Okay! I don't really get what's going on, but sure!"

Using Porta as a shield, Wise and Medhi beat a hasty retreat.

"Geez, those girls..."

"Oh no, they ran away! ...In that case, I'll have to start with you, Ma-kun. You were also part of this secret plan, weren't you?"

"Erk... That backfired... The whole keep-the-casino-secret-from-Mom plan was originally my idea, but... Oh, I know!"

Time to use what he'd learned.

"Hey, hey, Mommyyyy! How 'bout we just laugh this one off, okaaaay?" he pleaded in his most spoiled voice. That should do it. Mamako would definitely forgive—

"Hee-hee, not this time." *Grin.*

"Wait, she's not going into spoil mode?"

"But if you promise that next time you'll say 'Mommy, you should come with us!' then I might just forgive you."

"Mm? Maybe she is? ...What's going on?"

The heroic son had a long road ahead before he would truly understand the art of spoiling children.

Afterword

Hello, everyone. This is Dachima Inaka.

Thanks to your passionate support, the fourth volume is now on sale. I cannot thank you enough.

As a result, *Mom* is still going strong. She's on the cover of *Dragon Magazine*'s Thirtieth Anniversary issue (on sale the same day as this volume) and is the subject of a special feature article inside! And that's not all—there's a veritable parade of wonderful things happening, and I am so humbled by each and every one.

On the other hand, as the volume number goes up, I've become painfully aware of how hard writing mom light novels is.

My editor, K, compared it to "venturing forth into a field of virgin snow." We know there's a new land yet to be explored, but the path forward is unclear, and it's very hard to walk through it.

I know only too well what it feels like to be on a crazy adventure, one with a high chance of getting stranded somewhere.

But having started down this path, I must keep moving forward. Fueled by your support, once more I embark to realms unknown. As long as your love continues unabated, I will do so.

I'd like to dedicate this space to those involved with the book.

Iida Pochi., my editor, K, everyone involved with publication and sales, everyone who cosplayed as Mamako. Thank you all.

And to Meicha, who is doing the manga on the Young Ace Up website, here's to the beginning of what I hope is a long and fruitful partnership.

Not to change the subject, but my mother is also reading the manga. She drives a forklift around at work, spends her lunches and breaks reading light novels and manga, and sends e-mails not to the editorial department but directly to the author, demanding to know when the next volume will be released. She is a passionate (perhaps too passionate?) fan.

Just like Mamako, her son tends to find her enthusiasm a bit overwhelming...

Or perhaps I'm just writing this Mom light novel, as I should be.

Midwinter 2017, Dachima Inaka

"I'm just gonna go and enter this World Matriarchal Arts Tournament. I'll be back by dinner!"

Mamako Oosuki decides to participate in a tournament to determine who is the best mother in the world. Many different types of moms join in, but will Mamako emerge victorious? Will our protagonist, Masato, finally get the harem he's been hoping for?! He certainly is popular with mothers for some reason...

A cutting-edge momcom adventure!
Now it's the Tournament arc!

Do You Love Your Mom and Her Two-Hit Multi-Target Attacks?

VOLUME 5   Contents subject to change.

ON SALE SPRING 2020